DEADLY OBSESSION

Julie Ellis

SEVERN SH HOUSE

This first world edition published in Great Britain 1995 by
SEVERN HOUSE PUBLISHERS LTD of
9–15 High Street, Sutton, Surrey SM1 1DF.
First published in the USA 1996 by
SEVERN HOUSE PUBLISHERS INC. of
595 Madison Avenue, New York, NY 10022.

British Library Cataloguing in Publication Data

Ellis, Julie
    Deadly Obsession
    I. Title
    813.54 [F]

    ISBN 0-7278-4794-5

Typeset by Palimpsest Book Production Limited,
Polmont, Stirlingshire, Scotland.
Printed and bound in Great Britain by
Hartnolls Ltd, Bodmin, Cornwall.

Chapter One

The offices of *Manhattan Weekly* occupy the forty-third floor of a glass tower in the East Fifties. In the casually furnished lounge, where the coffee urn attracted its usual morning clientele, Laurie Roberts stood at a windowed area with a coffee-filled paper cup in hand and gazed out at the first flurries of a late January snow.

Born and raised in a small upstate New York town, Laurie normally enjoyed this view – the panorama of low and tall buildings, the delicate trappings of the bridges that formed a whimsical cut-out against the sky. But today she gazed at the view without seeing.

The magazine and her job as associate editor and occasional staff writer had been her life raft in the twenty-one months that she had been on the payroll. But today, she berated herself, she should have phoned in sick. How could she work with the calendar taunting her?

To look at the calendar was to remember the nightmare of two years ago today. The nightmare that left her widowed at twenty-seven after fourteen months of a near-perfect marriage.

In a surge of restlessness she crossed to the urn to refill her cup. This was her morning break, devoted to

1

coffee and the first section of the *New York Times*. The other three sections saw her through self-inflicted solitary dinners.

She ran one nervous hand through her short dark hair, that was a becoming frame for a face that was almost beautiful. Features delicate, skin a translucent cream. This morning the blue eyes, with the appealing wistfulness often associated with the near-sighted, were glazed over with pain.

She walked with the compulsive swiftness that prompted Ted Craig, a co-worker, to label her 'Miss Dynamo'. It was Ted, whom she had known at their midwest college, who had recruited her for this job. A fellow student in her English lit class, he had been pleased to have her instant friendship.

Whenever Mark and she had come into New York from their suburban Boston apartment, they had managed to have lunch or dinner with Ted.

Before Mark died, she had focused on a writing career. Two stories in *Alfred Hitchcock's Mystery Magazine*, two in *Ellery Queen*, plus the paperback novel that arrived in galleys the day before Mark died. She had been halfway through a second novel, but that was shelved. She was blocked; she couldn't write another word on the mystery that had fascinated her before Mark's death.

Laurie turned into her cubicle next to Ted's. She saw his tall, lean figure hunched over his desk. Jim Turner, their boss, had assigned Ted to write an article on battered wives, and he was totally involved in this.

Making an effort to avoid a confrontation with her desk calendar, Laurie sat down with her coffee, fished for the *Times* from the bottom drawer. In rushing for the bus this morning she had not even glanced at the headlines.

She unfolded the newspaper, flinched at what met her eyes.

'Body of Another Kidnap Victim Discovered in Aurelia'.

Laurie focused on the report of the finding of yet another small body in Aurelia, Alabama, where every mother walked in fear. In the past fifteen months sixteen young children had been kidnapped. With the latest body uncovered six were known to have been murdered. The others were still missing.

Laurie flinched at the jarring intrusion of the phone.

"Ted Craig," he answered briskly, and then his voice grew jubilant. "Angie, how are you?"

Angie was Ted's cherished older sister, Laurie recalled. She lived down in Alabama, didn't she?

"Angie, maybe he just wandered away." Ted's effort at calm seemed phoney. Laurie tensed. Angie lived in *Aurelia*. "That happens with little kids—"

Cold with alarm Laurie eavesdropped. Angie had been living in Aurelia for almost a year. Her husband was a social worker down there. They had one little boy. Tyrone. Involuntarily Laurie's eyes swept to the photograph of Tyrone on Ted's desk. No, she was being morbid. Nothing had happened to Angie's son.

"Angie, get hold of yourself." Ted's voice was taut. "The police will find Tyrone. He's adventurous – he wandered off somewhere. Is Bill there with you?" he asked, and then was silent for a moment. "Bill, tell me exactly what happened," he commanded when his brother-in-law was on the line.

Laurie sat immobile. Her eyes riveted now to the article on Aurelia in this morning's *Times*. Aurelia's citizens were simultaneously terrified and outraged. The whole country was emotionally involved in the trauma of the kidnappings and murders.

"Laurie—" Ted crossed to the low divider between their cubicles. "Angie's little boy has disappeared. He's been missing since five o'clock last night." Only Ted's eyes betrayed his anxiety. "They have a first floor apartment. Angie was watching him play from a window. The phone rang. She ran to answer. She came back in just two minutes, she said – and Tyrone was gone."

"He probably wandered away – after a ball or a stray dog," Laurie said quickly. "You know how kids—"

"He's been gone since five o'clock last night!" Ted broke in. "Angie said she and Bill have combed the area. The police have been out searching all night."

"You're going down to Aurelia," Laurie said. A sixth body had just been found, and now another child was missing.

Ted nodded. His face was grim. "I'll go home, pack a bag, and head for LaGuardia. There are flights out every hour. What kind of a monster is operating down there?" His voice soared in frustration. "What crazy gang is out to kill off the city's children?"

"You think it's a gang?"

"What else?" Ted countered. "Some insane cult, kidnapping a child every twenty-eight days. A child sacrificed to some diabolical ritual." He took a deep,

4

anguished breath. "Let them find Tyrone alive. He was six last week. I sent him a fire truck for his birthday. Laurie, tell Jim what's happened." He was checking his wallet now. "I'd better run to the bank before I head for the airport. And pray I can be of some use down there."

"Do you need money?" Laurie offered. She had not touched one cent of the insurance money Mark left her. To spend it was to recognize his death. In some obsessive way she felt that Mark was still with her as long as she didn't touch the insurance money. "I can loan you whatever you need—" This was an emergency; this was different. Ted was their friend.

"Thanks, Laurie. Credit cards will carry me through. You'd better remind Jim I may not be able to meet the deadline on that article on battered wives. I'll leave a note on his desk—"

"I'll remind him," Laurie promised. "He'll have somebody cover for you."

The office buzzed with the news that Ted's nephew – in Aurelia, Alabama – was missing. Laurie sat at her desk – too unnerved to work. All at once she felt herself racing back to those painful hours when she'd stood outside the low, sprawling suburban school where Mark had taught. Her car had stalled, making her late in arriving there.

Approaching the area she saw the line-up of police cars, emergency trucks, ambulances. And the huddled, frightened groups of parents who had been alerted to trouble. Mark and his class of fourth-graders, staying late to rehearse a play to be presented at assembly the next day, were held hostage by a psychotic intruder. If her car had not broken down, she would have been inside with them.

The police inched forward with tear gas.

"If you use gas, I'll kill six children!" the hostage-taker yelled in rage. "It'll be your fault if I have to do that!"

"What do you want?" the police chief finally asked.

"A helicopter to land on the rear grounds and to fly me to JFK. I want a plane there ready to fly me to Iran!" Inside the classroom one terrified child began to cry.

"Shut that brat up!" the intruder screamed. His voice reaching beyond the room to the terrified parents outside. The police were wary of moving in. "Shut her up, or I'll kill the little bitch!"

"Stop it!" Mark's voice ricocheted in the stunned silence. "Put down that gun!"

Four shots rang out. When the police rushed inside, they found the children safe. The intruder was dead. Mark was dying.

Laurie hunched over her computer and squinted into space. Like people throughout the country she had long been horrified by the kidnappings and murders of the children in the Southern city. Strung across a painful fifteen months. But for ten days now she had been haunted by a suspicion. *It was not just her mystery geared mind. It could be happening the way she envisioned it.*

She could pick up a telephone and call the police down in Aurelia and say, "Did you check this out?" But in cases like this the police were bombarded by cranks. That's what she would sound like to them. Another crank.

Last night she had read and re-read the newspaper stories she'd ripped out and saved. Searching for some clue that she was not alone in her suspicions. But nobody pounced on this as a motive. Ted had talked about a child being kidnapped every *twenty-eight days* – but it hadn't meant a thing to him.

With a need for action she left her desk and went out to the ladies' room. She'd go out for an early lunch. Jim Turner's secretary – arriving late because of a family funeral – was brushing her hair before the mirror.

"Did you hear about Ted's nephew?" Laurie asked her.

"What about him?" she asked with polite curiosity.

"Ted received a call from his sister an hour ago. His nephew – just six – disappeared last night. Ted's rushed down there to be with his sister."

"Did the kid run away from home or just wander away into the woods or something and got lost?" the secretary asked solicitously.

"Ted's sister lives in Aurelia, Alabama," Laurie said.

"Oh, God!" the secretary exclaimed. Laurie had captured her full attention. "They're afraid he was kidnapped by that gang that took the others?" The media, somehow, had assumed it was a gang operation.

"How do we know it's a gang?" Laurie pursued. "Didn't it hit you as strange that a child is snatched every twenty-eight days?"

"Yeah." She nodded vigorously. "Somebody is hung up on number twenty-eight."

Why couldn't Jim's secretary see what stared them in the face? Laurie churned with impatience. *Another woman ought to see it.*

Chapter Two

Laurie abandoned the prospect of an early lunch. She was too upset to eat. Now she struggled to concentrate on work. It was futile. She was obsessed by what was happening in Aurelia, Alabama.

On impulse she reached for the phone and dialled Ted's apartment. Maybe she could catch up with him before he left for the airport.

Drumming the fingers of one hand in impatience, she waited while the phone rang a dozen times. No answer. Ted was gone. Why hadn't she talked with him about her theory before he left? *It could be happening that way.* She felt like one of those people who hear a woman screaming in the middle of the night and don't even bother to investigate, she chastised herself.

All at once she knew she could not remain a bystander. Not when such conviction clutched at her. She swept the notes for her current assignment before her into a folder, thrust the folder into her top desk drawer. This was a month-long project. She could steal time away from it and still make her deadline.

In a sudden decision she prepared to leave for lunch. A long lunch, she surmised, considering her objective. Nobody would question her absence. They would assume she was out on research. She would be. But not on her current assignment.

Her briefcase under one arm, Laurie strode south along people-cluttered Madison Avenue, where occasional flurries of snow seemed to elicit delight from more adventurous pedestrians. This morning she was hardly aware of her surroundings.

The disappearance of Ted's nephew had made the Aurelia kidnappings painfully personal. Why hadn't she talked with him about her suspicions before he left? Now he was *en route* to Aurelia.

Was she way off base? Had this possibility been explored and discarded? No, she was convinced. No word along those lines had leaked into the news accounts of the happenings in Aurelia. There would have been *some* word.

At Forty-Second Street she turned west to the New York Public Library. Rarely did this monumental store-house of information fail her. She hurried up the stairs at the Forty-Second Street entrance and walked inside to the bank of elevators. Her mind racing all the while.

If she still felt as sure after double-checking the facts that her theory had validity, then she must try to talk Jim into sending her down to Aurelia to do a story on the kidnappings and murders. It was a story that should be written by a woman.

Laurie rushed into an elevator, rode up to the third floor. She hurried from the elevator, down the long corridor to Room 315. Mentally packing a suitcase as she walked. Instinct told her she would be *en route* to Aurelia within twenty-four hours. Laurie valued instinct.

In Room 315 she queued up at the Information Counter to enquire if the library stored microfilm copies of the back issues of the *Aurelia Constitution.*

"I'm looking for last year and the year before that," she explained.

"We don't have them here," the man behind the counter told her regretfully.

"Do you know where I might find them?" Laurie was disappointed. "Would they be at the Annex or one of the branch libraries?"

"No. You might try the college libraries," he suggested after a moment of cogitation. "I suspect that Yale will have them on file."

"Thank you."

Yale would mean a trip up to New Haven. A delay to be avoided if humanly possible. Again, instinct shoved her into action. She hurried from the immense card file mausoleum down the marble hall to the bank of telephones opposite the elevators.

Tyrone had been missing since five o'clock last night. The young boy whose body had just been discovered had been missing three months. The coroner's report stated that he had been killed within four to six days after his disappearance. If Tyrone was to be found alive, it must be soon.

Laurie slid into an empty phone booth, dug into her purse for a coin. From Information she acquired a number for Columbia College. She had taken an evening course there last term. More to keep herself occupied two evenings a week than from a thirst for knowledge.

She dialled the main library at Columbia, impatient

to move into action. Columbia was a familiar locale. Their research materials impressive.

"Are you a student here?" the voice at the other end enquired when she asked about the availability of the Aurelia newspapers for the past eighteen months.

"Not at the present," Laurie admitted.

"If the newspapers are not available at the Forty-Second Street library, they can give you an admittance card that will be good for two weeks of guest privileges in our microfilm room. We have back issues on microfilm. Just bring the card to Butler Hall. You'll be given a Columbia card that provides access to the microfilm room at Butler."

"Thank you." Relief surged through her. She would not have to make the trek to Yale.

She backtracked to Room 315. Fretting at having to wait in line again. But this was surely one of the great libraries of the world. Naturally it was heavily patronized. Churning with impatience she plotted her course. She would go up to the Columbia library as soon as she had the guest card in her hand. But first she must talk to Jim. Sell him on sending her down to Aurelia to research the article.

Jim was familiar with her writing background, aside from what she had done on the magazine. While it was light, it was in the mystery field. This should be a plus for writing an article on the Aurelia nightmare. That would be the title, she decided: 'The Aurelia Nightmare'.

At last, with guest card stashed in her briefcase, Laurie headed again for the phones. She dialled the office, hoping Jim had not dashed off on another three-hour business lunch. If she handled this right, she could be in Aurelia tonight.

Jim's secretary located him for Laurie. He was in the Art Department.

"Ted asked me to be sure you noticed the note he left for you," Laurie said. "Did you see it?"

"Yes." Jim was sombre. "Terrible thing to have happened. Terrible for all the kids involved—"

"I'd like to go down there and do a feature article about it. 'The Aurelia Nightmare'," she pitched. Her heart was pounding. She was still a lower echelon editor, assigned mainly to research. She wanted to write this one. "It could be powerful, Jim. Zooming in on the fears of the mothers of the city. What's in their minds, how they cope from day to day. This is a situation that everybody can relate to. It could happen anywhere. Even right here in Manhattan."

"We're not running a women's magazine," Jim reminded. "It would have to be a hard-driving crime story. I'm not sure that you—"

"Crime with heavy human interest," Laurie pinpointed. "All crime brings out human emotions; but when children are involved, it's much more poignant."

"It could be dangerous," Jim hedged, "if you start digging too close to the truth. It should be handled by somebody with a crime writing background."

"I have background in crime writing!" She'd die if Jim sent somebody else down to Aurelia. "I've worked in that area on the magazine, too." She hesitated. "If I bring in a story you don't want to use, throw me off salary for the time I'm down there," she cajoled. "I'll pay my own expenses if you reject the article."

Jim chuckled. "That kind of enthusiasm I can't turn down. But remember, Laurie. I may want to put a re-write person on it. I can't make promises. Bring me back something with drama and heart. That sells magazines."

"It'll be a blockbuster," she promised, giddy with success. She needed an assignment to use as a wedge down in Aurelia. Her reason for asking questions.

"When do you want to leave?"

"Tonight," Laurie told him. "Right now I'm on my way up to Columbia College to read the back issues of the *Aurelia Constitution* for the past fifteen months."

"We'll go for a four-day expense account," Jim stipulated. "If you stay longer, you're on your own."

Laurie left the library and hurried to Times Square to take a train uptown. Living in mid-Manhattan she rarely travelled on the trains. She loathed the noise, the crowds, the hassling for seats. Today she was grateful for the speed of the subway trains. In about twelve minutes she was emerging from the Columbia University station into the bleak, cold air.

She paused in reflection while throngs of students trudged past her, heading for the various fast food spots sprinkled along Broadway. Reminding Laurie that she had not lunched, and breakfast had been only juice and coffee. She would be holed up in the microfilm room at Butler for hours, she surmised. Go somewhere for a sandwich.

She dashed into a McDonald's, spied an empty stool, and ordered a burger and coffee. Waiting to be served she searched her mind for the married name of Ted's sister down in Aurelia. Chastising herself for not having asked Ted before he left. Never mind that oversight. She'd locate Ted's sister in Aurelia.

Even while Ted had been talking on the phone this morning with his sister and brother-in-law, she had known she would try to persuade Jim to send her down to Aurelia on the kidnap and murder story. She didn't dare tell Jim she harboured a personal theory about who was responsible for the deaths of those children. Jim would jump to the conclusion that she was researching for a future novel.

Again she asked herself if the police had explored this theory and rejected it. Again, she discarded such speculation. In all these months, if it had come up, some reporter would have used it in a story.

She ate her burger and coffee without tasting. Her mind turning over every aspect of the case. From the moment the 'Aurelia Nightmare' became nationwide news, she had been emotionally embroiled. Here again – as with Mark – were children in danger.

The police – the city administration – were desperate to stop the kidnappings and murders. The entire city was caught up in the hunt. Seemingly no possibility was being ignored. *Could they be overlooking the most obvious clue?*

Laurie left the McDonald's and crossed the wide street to the entrance to the campus. Columbia was a study in grey. Winter-barren trees, grey buildings against a grey sky. She asked a pair of down-jacketed students the direction to Butler Library.

Inside Butler, a guard sent her to the office where the card she had received at the Forty-Second Street

15

Library was exchanged for a card that would give her access to the microfilm room.

For four hours Laurie pored over back issues of the *Aurelia Constitution*. Her eyes strained, her throat dry, she made copies of every item, no matter how repetitive, how brief.

Criminal minds from widely scattered areas of the country had gone to Aurelia to help fight the massacre of the city's children. A male psychic had been brought down from Chicago to work with the police. The Mayor had ordered house-to-house searches.

Yet instinct continued to tell Laurie that one approach was not being pursued. A million-to-one shot – *but it could be happening the way she suspected.*

At a few minutes past six, breathless and with overnight bag and briefcase in tow, Laurie strode toward West Forty-Second Street to wait for the bus that would take her to LaGuardia. Before midnight – if she could get a seat on the plane, by virtue of a cancellation – she would be in Aurelia. Another major city, she remembered Ted's saying, where no woman should move about alone after dark.

Chapter Three

The 'Please Fasten Seat Belts' sign was lighted. The plane was taxiing down the runway preparing for take-off. Laurie stared out the window, grateful that a seat had become available. She would arrive in Aurelia shortly past ten pm.

The plane lifted. The landscape tilted. Normally at this point on a plane Laurie switched her gaze to some stable area within the cabin. Tonight the tilting landscape signified the horror down in Aurelia. This was the way the world appeared to mothers fearful of allowing children out of their sight. A tilted world where a killer – or killers – roamed on a trail of horror.

It could be a couple, Laurie considered. A deranged woman and her man. Now she forced herself to flip open the magazine she had picked up at a newsstand in the airport.

It seemed to Laurie that they had been airborne only a few minutes when the food parade began to invade the aisle. The appearance of the dinner trays, the smiling faces of the stewardesses were oddly reassuring. For the two hours plus between LaGuardia and the Aurelia airport they existed in a vacuum where nothing horrible could occur.

Tyrone *could* have wandered away. Ted said there were woods behind the apartment house where his sister and her family lived. A six-year-old could have got lost. But the searchers would have found him by now, her mind rejected. And he was too young to be a runaway.

"My mother tells me I always fly Delta because of the pecan pie you serve for dessert," the passenger in the aisle seat teased the stewardess. A warmth in his voice drew a glance from Laurie. He was young and good-looking. Her eyes grazed the attaché case deposited on the empty seat between them. A young executive on a business trip, she assessed. "I'm disappointed you're not serving mint juleps."

"We'll see what we can do about the mint juleps the next time you fly Delta," the stewardess laughed.

"I must have been an Alabaman in another life." He turned to Laurie with the friendliness of a St Bernard as the stewardess moved on. "Are you from Alabama?"

"I'm from upstate New York. I live in New York City now." How could she be annoyed at this good-humoured effort at conversation? He wasn't trying for a pick-up.

"I'm from Albany, New York." His brown eyes lighted when he smiled. His features were almost movie star handsome. "What about you?"

"A town you never heard of," Laurie guessed. "Cambridge."

"Sure I know Cambridge, New York. Some of the best trout fishing in the country up there. I seem to recall a hotel that claims it's the 'home of pie à la mode'," he said.

"The Cambridge Hotel," Laurie identified. She had not been in Cambridge since her sophomore year in college, when she was called home to the first tragedy in her life. Her mother and father had been killed in a head-on collision. That was one of the reasons she never drank. The driver of the killer car had been drunk. "The hotel is still there."

"I went to med school in New York City," he told her while he dug into the plastic tray of food before him. "I'm a resident now in a hospital down in Aurelia. Paul Norman," he introduced himself.

"Laurie Roberts," she said. "It's horrible what's happening down in Aurelia." He was a doctor. Would he think she was crazy if she told him her theory about the murders? But she would hug these suspicions to herself for now. The police would think she was a meddling magazine writer out for a sensational story. "Have there been new developments? I read in this morning's papers about another body being found."

"Another child is missing," he reported sombrely. "Just like the others. Vanished into thin air. I heard about it when I called a friend down in Aurelia this morning. He's covering for me at the hospital," he explained with a grin. "I wanted to put his mind at rest and let him know I'll be back on schedule. I flew up to New York four days ago for a buddy's wedding."

"The child your friend told you about is the nephew of a friend of mine." Laurie felt brushed by cold. But Angie's child was *missing*, not dead. "We work on the same magazine. His sister phoned from Aurelia. His nephew has been missing since five o'clock yesterday afternoon."

Paul's dark eyes were troubled when he said, "The police are breaking their backs but coming up with nothing. There's never been a case in the city so tough to crack. And every twenty-eight days, like clockwork, another child disappears." Laurie's throat tightened with excitement as Paul talked. He was a doctor. Couldn't he see what she saw in this? *A motive.* "Five of the children found murdered. Six," he corrected himself. "God, everybody feels so helpless!"

"Do you remember those older women that were murdered down in Georgia some years ago? The police never found the murderer in that case, either," Laurie recalled.

"Seven of them, wasn't it? I believe one of his intended victims survived. But that stopped. This case just goes on and on. If I were a family man, I think I'd send my kids out of the state." Paul Norman wasn't married. Why should that please her?

"They've all been young children of about five or six," Laurie said.

"So far it's been young children," Paul conceded. "But what's to guarantee that he – or they – won't start picking on children from a different age group or a different area. We don't know anything," he said in a frustration that seemed almost personal. Paul Norman was a warm, caring man, Laurie decided. "We don't know the motivation behind the kidnapper-killer's mind."

They paused while the stewardess poured coffee for them. Then Paul switched the conversation into lighter, more personal channels.

"You said you work on a magazine. Are you going

20

to Aurelia on business?" He was genuinely interested, Laurie thought.

"I'm going down there for the magazine," she admitted without being specific. She recoiled from explaining that she was to research the murders. "I've never been to Aurelia. I was glad of an excuse to come down." She was *en route* to Aurelia to pursue her theory about the murders. To help find Tyrone while he was still alive. How many crackpots called the police each day with 'theories'? How many wrote letters to the local newspapers?

"Why don't we have dinner tomorrow night?" Paul asked. She had intercepted his covert glance at her ringless left hand. She wore her wedding band on her right hand since Mark's death. "I'll tell you all about the city. I'm a real Aurelia buff. After all, we're both from upstate New York," he laughed. "I owe it to you."

"I'd like that," she said, startling herself. In the two years since Mark's death she had gone out with no one. Why had she agreed to have dinner with an absolute stranger? She had filled her nights with classes, exercise groups, occasional splurges on theatre and ballet tickets. She had been grateful to be occupied by day at the magazine.

For the remainder of the flight into Aurelia Paul Norman amused her with med school and hospital internship humour. He was clearly not one of those who had gone into medicine in order to have income tax problems. He planned on setting up practice in a small town and devoting his life to serving.

"An old-fashioned GP?" Laurie asked with respect.

"A new-fashioned pediatrician." Paul chuckled. "One who'll make house calls. I know the routine about how a doctor can serve ten times as many patients if he stays in his office. But if I have a patient running a temperature of one hundred and three, I don't want his parents dragging him to my office. I mean to go to him."

Laurie was surprised when the 'Please Fasten Seat Belts' sign flashed again. They were preparing to land. The trip had seemed so brief in Paul Norman's company. But was she making a mistake in agreeing to have dinner with him tomorrow night? Oh, why not, she defended her impulsive decision. She had been existing in a vacuum for two years.

"Where are you staying in Aurelia?" Paul asked while they stood waiting to leave the plane.

"I made reservations at a downtown motel," she told him. Guaranteed reservations. The magazine would pay her expenses if Jim accepted the article, but he would balk at her staying at one of the posh hotels for which Aurelia was famous. "I wanted to be near everything." *What was everything?*

Ostensibly she was here to do a magazine article. Yet it wasn't the desire to write the article that sent her racing down here. Why did she feel this commitment to help solve the crime?

She wasn't a detective. She had no training for that kind of work. The police were bombarded by people sure they could solve these murders. It was always that way when something awful happened. It would be absurd to try to voice her suspicions.

"I have my car at the airport parking lot," Paul

22

intruded on her introspection. "Let's collect our luggage from the conveyor belt, and I'll drive you to your motel."

"Lovely," she accepted, yet she was uneasy. Was she being naïve? She didn't know Paul Norman. She didn't even know that he was a doctor. With all that was happening in Aurelia, was she stupid to trust a stranger?

"First, let me phone the hospital," Paul said when they were walking through the vast airport to the luggage bay. "I like to put myself on call in case of an emergency, even though I don't go on duty until tomorrow morning." He grinned. "I'm a compulsive doctor. The training I acquire at the hospital emergency room is something I'll never get in private practice."

Laurie stood by while Paul phoned the hospital. Listening to the conversation, she felt a faint guilt. He was Paul Norman, MD; no doubt lingered in her mind now.

She suppressed an impulse to talk further about the Aurelia kidnappings and murders. Tomorrow night over dinner she would make a stab at it. She suspected that Paul Norman would not dismiss her as a neurotic woman or a publicity seeker. He would understand what she had to say.

They picked up Paul's car. He drove her into town, pointing out landmarks along the way. He was proud of Aurelia Memorial Hospital, where he had served his internship and was now a pediatrics resident.

"We care for a special segment of the population," he said with satisfaction. "We reach out to low-income families. The ones with no health insurance and little

23

cash. One of the kids – her body was found last October – was my patient. I pulled her through a bad case of pneumonia. When she was better, she came to the clinic with a bag full of chocolate chip cookies for me." His eyes were pained. "At the hospital we feel hard hit. *Who's killing the kids of Aurelia, Alabama?*"

Paul drove her up to the motel entrance, brought out her case from the trunk, and put her into the hands of a porter.

"I'll pick you up in the lobby tomorrow night at six," he said. "Don't go out after dark," he exhorted. "Not alone."

Chapter Four

Feeling like an actress in a play, Laurie unpacked her case. Was it too late to try to reach Ted, she asked herself while she struggled with the motel hangers. Tonight this seemed an irritating chore. No, it wasn't too late. Ted would want to hear from her.

Ted wouldn't be staying at a hotel, she reasoned. He would be at his sister's apartment. He always stayed with Angie when he was in Aurelia. At a time like this he'd want to be underfoot in case of some development.

She didn't know the phone number at his sister's apartment, Laurie remembered in fresh frustration. Why hadn't she picked this up at the office before she rushed off to the airport? It was time to organize her thinking.

Would Ted think she was crazy to come chasing down here this way? She had no plotted plan of action. Only an instinct – and an obsession to help. She was here in Aurelia on assignment. That made her pretense legitimate.

Go down to the lobby, pick up this evening's newspapers. Tyrone's name would be there. She didn't know Angie's married name. Hopefully Angie had a listed phone number. If not, try the police. If that failed phone the magazine first thing in the morning.

She tossed small items into a dresser drawer, reached for her room key, and headed for the lobby. She didn't want to wait until tomorrow morning to track down Ted. She was here. She wanted to talk to him tonight. Time was precious.

In the lobby Laurie sought out the newsstand. She bought the evening newspapers. Waiting for change she remembered she had forgot to pack a toothbrush and toothpaste. Both were available at the newsstand.

Newspapers tucked under one arm Laurie returned to her room in haste. She deposited the newspapers on one of the double beds that are standard equipment in motel rooms and returned to double-lock the door and slide the chain into place. Was there a spot left in this world where people were not security conscious?

She reached for one newspaper. Tyrone's photograph leapt at her from above a centre double-column spread. The same appealing photograph that Ted kept on his desk accompanied the article. Luckily Tyrone's surname was mentioned in the report, so she knew where to start.

Laurie also scanned what little there was to be told about Tyrone's disappearance, together with a reprisal of what had been happening in Aurelia for the past fifteen months. Poor little Tyrone. *Was he all right*?

Laurie reached for the telephone book on the lower shelf of the night table. She flipped the pages until she reached 'Randolph'. At least half a dozen Randolph's were listed. None with the first name of Angela.

The first Randolph she called was annoyed at being

26

disturbed at past eleven at night. Laurie suppressed her guilt, apologized, and tried the next Randolph. She allowed the phone to ring a dozen times. Nobody answered.

Someone would be at Tyrone's apartment, Laurie reasoned. Unless something had happened. Something good, she soothed herself. Like maybe Tyrone did just wander away and somebody had found him. Yet instinct demanded she try the other numbers listed under 'Randolph'.

She sat at the edge of the bed and dialled again. A babysitter responded.

"No. Nobody named Angela lives here," a cheerful teenager told her.

Not until the fourth call did she reach the Randolph family she sought.

"Hello," a strained masculine voice answered at the other end. A familiar voice.

"Ted," Laurie said with relief.

"Laurie?" Ted was astonished. "Something go haywire at the magazine? I left a note for Jim—"

"No, it's not the magazine," Laurie hastened to reassure him. "Jim knows you're in Aurelia. I'm down here, too. I talked Jim into letting me come down here to work up a story about the kidnappings." She couldn't bring herself to say 'the murdered children'.

"Oh, for God's sake, Laurie!" Ted was furious.

"Ted, listen to me," she pleaded. "I'm not trying to use your contacts to dig up a great story. You know how I feel about children. You know how Mark died. I had to come down here. Ted, I have a wild theory about what's happening with the children,"

27

she blurted out. "I realize the police would think I'm off the wall—"

"Where are you?"

"At a downtown motel," she told him. "Has there been any news of Tyrone?"

"No." Ted's voice cracked. "Angie's under sedation. Bill's just holding himself together. We don't know where Tyrone is. We don't know if he's alive."

"He's alive." Laurie was insistent. "Ted, remember the pattern. The children are kept alive for several days."

"The coroner's reports on the bodies discovered so far indicate the murders took place from four to six days after the kidnapping." Ted corroborated what she had read. "Tyrone was kidnapped yesterday afternoon."

"There's time to find him," Laurie pinpointed. "Ted, the restaurant here is open late. Do you want to come over and talk? I have a strong hunch about what's happening. I know I sound like the crackpot of the year . . ."

"I'll meet you in the restaurant in fifteen minutes," Ted said without hesitation, then took down the name of the motel. "I'm not doing any good sitting around the apartment worrying about Tyrone. If you've got a theory, Laurie, let's explore it."

Chapter Five

Laurie sat at a table in the attractive motel restaurant and watched for Ted's arrival. Her mind focused on Tyrone. What anguish his parents must be enduring! Such a little boy and missing since five o'clock yesterday afternoon. The discovery of another body made Tyrone's disappearance doubly painful for his parents.

She straightened up in her chair at the sight of Ted striding towards her.

"Hey, forgive me for yelling at you like that," he apologized, grasping her hand in his as he sat down. "I feel so damn frustrated at not being able to do anything."

"Ted, I spent four hours today copying every article I could find on the kidnappings in the microfilm files of the Aurelia *Constitution*. Some of the children could be alive."

"Could be," Ted agreed. "We don't know. The police don't know. They're not optimistic as bodies keep turning up. Nobody has tried to contact any of the families. It's been a complete blackout since the first child disappeared."

A waiter arrived. Laurie and Ted ordered to give

themselves the privilege of lingering here. The tables were sparsely occupied. They could talk in privacy.

"All kinds of theories have been explored," Ted reminded her. "A lot of way-out, impossible ideas. The police are desperate. The city is desperate."

"My theory is way out," Laurie warned.

"Lay it out for me," Ted ordered.

Self-conscious but determined, Laurie gave him her version of what was happening. Ted seemed glassy-eyed with shock.

"You don't believe there's a chance it could be going down like that," she said in disappointment.

"I can *believe* it," Ted said. "But how will we ever track down a suspect?"

"You think we should go to the police?" A kind of relief washed over Laurie. They would know how to follow up this kind of theory. The police were knowledgeable, crime-oriented. She groped in the dark.

"Laurie, they'll think you're an opportunist," Ted voiced her own suspicions. "A big-city young writer comes to Aurelia to try out a plot for a mystery novel she's weaving. That's how it'll look to anybody else. They don't know you the way I do. Laurie, they'll be turned off."

"They're working with a psychic," Laurie persisted.

"A mystery writer is too far out," Ted said bluntly. "That belongs to 1940s movies."

"Ted, I'm not a mystery writer now."

"They'll check you out. You've written for mystery magazines. You've had a paperback mystery published. They'll figure you're here to do an article for the magazine, but that you mean to use it as a springboard to a novel."

"But it could be happening this way!"

"Laurie, they've got just so much manpower. This won't seem worth taking detectives off something else." He hesitated. "I'm not sure if I should even discuss this with Angie and Bill."

"Your sister is a woman," Laurie said stubbornly. "She'll see what I'm trying to say." *They might find Tyrone alive if they followed her instinct.*

"Look, what can we do to follow through on this on our own?" Ted demanded. "I can't sit around that apartment all day. I have to do something."

"Let me interview some of the mothers of children who're missing or dead," Laurie said after a moment.

"What good will that do? Except to give you material for an article." Ted's eyes were cynical.

"Ted, do you believe that's why I'm down here?" Laurie accused. "The article is a wedge. I need a reason to be here."

"I'm sorry, Laurie. I'm shooting off my mouth again. But when I think of Tyrone out there with God only knows what lunatic . . ." Ted shook his head in anguish. "All those poor little kids."

"I don't know what I'm looking for – I'm not a detective. But I have a hunch that, talking with some of the mothers, I might stumble on a lead."

Tomorrow night she'd talk with Paul Norman. Paul, Ted, and she would try to track down the suspect she was sure was out to murder a young child every twenty-eight days, as had happened for agonizing months. Let them catch her – if *she* was right – before she tried again. While Tyrone – and with God's help – some of the other children still lived.

"Anybody else you want to talk to?" In desperation Ted grasped at this meagre hope, Laurie recognized in compassion.

"You said your sister's husband is a social worker." Laurie was reaching out for help. "Would he know a psychologist? Someone private that we could talk to?"

"It's likely." Ted squinted in thought. "Yeah! I remember meeting some psychologist at a Christmas party at their apartment last year. I'll set up a meeting for you as soon as I can. Tomorrow if possible. I'll pick you up here tomorrow morning at nine. Laurie, let's try every damn way we can to find Tyrone."

Chapter Six

The sleet began to fall just past midnight. The sky was wine-red with promise of more. Behind the wheel of the long-haul truck that sped over the empty highway towards Aurelia, Gus Johnson shifted his two hundred pound six foot two frame in nervous unease. His partner slept. They had been on the road for seventy-two hours.

Christ, he had been jumpy as hell since this morning, Gus admitted to himself. Ever since Chuck parked the truck in the parking area of the diner and they walked inside. Never guessing what was going to smack him right in the eye.

This was the diner they always tried to reach in time for breakfast. He was already envisaging a plate piled up with pancakes, fried eggs and bacon. The morning cook knew he hated bacon when it was burnt to a crisp. Just beginning to curl up, sizzling in the fat – that was the way he liked it.

They sat in a booth and kidded around with that frizzy-haired blonde waitress who always wore a uniform two sizes too small for her. And then Chuck leaned back and picked up a newspaper from the counter beside the cash register that sat behind their booth. The newspapers were there to be read; they were not on sale.

All Chuck cared about were the basketball scores. He fished out the sports section and threw the rest of the newspaper on the seat beside him. With the front page staring up with that headline Gus had not expected to see:

'Sixth Body Found in Aurelia'.

He couldn't believe it. How did the fuzz find the body? Who went diggin' in the middle of the cold, hard fields this time of year? He didn't think they'd ever find this one. All the farmer put in those acres was alfalfa. No need to go diggin' down three feet into the dirt. The kid should have stayed there forever, until there was nothing left but bones.

Chuck couldn't figure out why Gus was suddenly so pissed off. He'd sent his breakfast back, complaining the pancakes were burnt, the eggs too hard, the bacon overdone. His hand shook so much when he lifted the coffee cup to his mouth he'd sloshed the coffee into the saucer.

But nobody knew. He didn't have to worry. *Nobody knew*.

"Hey, Chuck! Wake up." In a few minutes they'd be pulling into the terminal. He'd pick up a six-pack and head out to the farm on the Harley. In the back of the truck was the fancy dressed doll they'd seen in a store window in New Orleans. It oughta make Lottie happy. Cost him a bundle.

"What the hell's the matter with you, Gus?" Chuck grimaced in irritation as he stretched into wakefulness. "You used to be such a nice guy. The last year or so you ain't nobody's friend. Wakin' me up like you hoped I'd have a stroke from the shock. What's eatin' you these days?"

"Nothin's eatin' me!" Gus snarled. "You tired of me, go drive with somebody else."

"Maybe I will," Chuck shot back. "You useda be fun on the road. I mean, we had a lotta laughs. You sure changed, man."

"I ain't changed." Suddenly Gus was uneasy. "I'm just gettin' tired of these long hauls. Lottie complains all the time about how I ain't ever home."

"But when you're home, you make up." All at once Chuck was good-humoured. "The little woman keeps you happy, don't she?" Chuck had never met Lottie.

"Yeah, sure."

"Gus, you ain't still upset about—" Chuck was sombre.

"I ain't upset about nothin'," Gus shut him up. Why the hell had he shot off his mouth to Chuck when they first started drivin' together? "Lottie and me – we're doin' just fine." He didn't want to think about that vacation up in South Carolina, when they went to visit Lottie's aunt. That was when everythin' started goin' bad.

Gus didn't want to talk any more. He didn't trust anybody. Not even his partner. He couldn't afford to trust anybody.

At the terminal Gus checked out as fast as possible. It would be a bitch on the Harley in this sleet, he thought while he wrapped the package for Lottie in plastic before attaching it to the luggage rack.

Still, he liked the sense of power he got riding in the wind.

Lottie didn't read the newspapers. All she read was the clothing catalogues. She wouldn't know about the creepy kid's body. She didn't know about any of 'em. Lottie wouldn't give him no trouble.

He was doin' it all for her, wasn't he? She made him do it.

Chapter Seven

Laurie sat up in bed until past three am, searching for something she might have missed in the copies of the microfilmed newspaper articles. When she was about to capitulate, she homed in on the excerpt reporting that some of the bodies indicated they had received care before their deaths.

Someone – the kidnapper – loved children, Laurie told herself with fresh conviction. But some crazy turn of mind made her kill them. Or did her husband – or man friend – kill them?

These children had not been tortured before they were murdered, Laurie remembered, so was the actual murder in these cases a sadistic sexual turn-on for a psychotic couple? That would be a course the police would follow, Laurie reasoned.

She clung to the regularity with which the kidnappings occurred. Every twenty-eight days. A definite cycle. No ritual, her mind insisted. Nature.

She stashed away the copies she had made in the microfilm room at Butler and prepared for bed. Her head ached from the hours devoted to re-reading the eye-straining copies of the newspaper articles. She was stiff from tension. Too keyed up to fall right asleep, she guessed. Too much had happened today.

She set the alarm for eight am. That would give her time for a long hot shower and a shampoo before she went down to the restaurant to meet Ted. On impulse she went to the door to make sure the chain was in place, then crossed to the window to gaze out through a slit in the drapes. The sleet had changed to snow. Silver dollar sized flakes were plummeting from the snow-heavy sky and sticking.

Laurie slid beneath the blankets. Somehow, she had always envisaged Aurelia as being eternally warm, but it wasn't now.

Outside in the corridor a pair of lusty male voices erupted into a college song.

"Shut up!" another male voice hissed. "You want us to get thrown out of here?"

Laurie was sliding into her coat, grateful that New York weather had necessitated her wearing this, when the phone rang. She hurried to respond.

"I'm a few minutes early," Ted said. "I'll be waiting in the restaurant."

"I'll be right there," Laurie told him.

She found Ted at the table where they had sat last night. This morning every table was occupied. Breakfast was being served buffet style.

"I'll bring a tray for both of us," Ted offered. "What would you like?"

"Just juice and coffee." The almost convivial atmosphere in the restaurant disturbed her. Didn't these people know what was happening to the children in

Aurelia? Then she noticed the name tags worn by many of the diners and realized this was a convention group.

Laurie sat back in the comfortable chair and suppressed a stream of yawns. Less than five hours sleep had not been sufficient. Panic touched her with reproachful fingers. She had come down to Aurelia with a conviction – but without any real plan about how to follow up on what she believed was happening.

She felt a personal responsibility for discovering Tyrone while he was still alive. There would not be another child kidnapped for another twenty-four days if the pattern was followed. But what about those whose bodies had not been recovered? Were any of them still alive?

Ted returned to their table with a loaded tray. Orange juice, scrambled eggs, toast and coffee for the two of them.

"You need a substantial breakfast," Ted said crisply, distributing the contents of the tray. "I was at the police station this morning," he reported. "They've found the fire truck Tyrone was playing with when he disappeared." Ted flinched. "The one I sent him from New York."

"Where was it?"

"In a clump of bushes fifty feet from the entrance to the apartment," Ted told her. "He must have been taken by someone who looked as though he belonged on the grounds. With everybody so frightened, a stranger would have sent the kids scurrying into the apartment lobby."

"You said Angie was at the window looking for

Tyrone at five o'clock. At this time of year it's almost dark by then. A stranger could have wandered into the housing estate without being noticed. A woman," Laurie said with excitement coating her voice. "To a child that means somebody's mother. She may have promised him sweets or a biscuit or ice-cream. He wouldn't be afraid. He'd associate a friendly woman with his mother. In the dark she could have just walked off with him."

"The police made a door-to-door search. They've questioned every man, woman, and child in every apartment in every area within the city limits," Ted said. His eyes searched Laurie's. Hoping she would come up with a miracle.

"Did you set up a meeting with the psychologist?" Laurie asked.

"He's out of town today. We'll see him tomorrow for sure. Bill promises."

"Did you set up interviews for me?" Laurie pursued. Moving ahead on instinct. All she had working for her, she admitted, was a conviction and instinct.

"I've set up three. Two with mothers whose children's bodies have been discovered. Another with a child still missing. Laurie, they've been through hell. I don't know that it's right to put them through more."

"They want to see the murders stopped, Ted. They'll understand that we want to help." Yet she recoiled from intruding on their grief.

"They've been interviewed endlessly by the police," he cautioned. "If they're impatient, you must understand."

"You're sure Bill can arrange a meeting with his psychologist friend for tomorrow?" *They couldn't wait.*

"No problem. We'll have lunch together. The four of us." Ted toyed with his scrambled eggs. "You're searching for a profile?"

"I'm looking for support in what I believe." Laurie leaned forward, her voice low. "The children who were murdered were killed in different fashions. I want to know if a psychotic killer would follow a pattern. I just can't believe we're looking for a psychotic killer. The children whose bodies were found had been well cared for, and they had not been killed immediately after abduction. Someone felt affection towards them. And then something happened . . ."

"I'm trying to persuade Bill to go back into his office. It's futile for him to stay home. Angie's mother has come over from Opelike to be with her."

"Did you tell Angie what I suspect?" Laurie asked.

Ted shook his head. "She's too distraught even to discuss it."

Laurie was relieved that Ted had not told Angie. That would lay an extra responsibility on her. She prayed she could help find Tyrone. She didn't know that she could.

"I'm having dinner tonight with a doctor I met on the plane." Paul would do anything he could to help. He was concerned about the children. "Paul Norman. He's a resident at Aurelia Memorial. The hospital that services the area where some of the children have gone missing," she emphasized. "He's a pediatrician." Paul was honestly involved with the children. He'd want to help.

"What do you expect to learn from him?" Ted asked.

"He can help us. Ted, it *could* be the way I see it. A woman who's lost a child in an accident or by illness is desperate to become pregnant again. She realizes each month – a lot of women have a twenty-eight day cycle – that she's not carrying a child, and goes berserk. If I can persuade Paul Norman that we're on to something, he'll be able to get us the names of every child who died in his hospital within a ninety day period of the first kidnapping. Then we'll follow up on the mothers."

"Laurie, have you any idea how long that'll take?" A nerve quivered in Ted's right eyelid. "We don't know how long Tyrone – how long he'll stay alive."

"We'll work around the clock if we must," Laura said. "Bill will help, won't he?"

"Of course he'll help." Ted was brusque in his anxiety. "Nail down that list, Laurie!"

Chapter Eight

The alarm was a raucous intrusion on this morning that still wore the look of night. Without opening his eyes Paul reached over and groped for the alarm, found the offending buzzer, and shut it up.

Rolling over onto his back for a final few moments of rest he geared himself for the fast morning routine of shower, shave, breakfast, and dash to the hospital. No breakfast at home today, he decided, ignoring his budget. He would have breakfast at the hospital. He was in no mood for domesticity. He had been short-changed on sleep last night.

He had gone to bed as soon as he reached the apartment, Paul recalled. He had not fallen asleep for almost two hours. He'd blamed it on the two cups of coffee he had consumed on arriving at the apartment. It wasn't the coffee. He kept thinking about Laurie Roberts.

If she was down here on an assignment, she wouldn't be here long. So he'd see her while she was in Aurelia. That didn't constitute a commitment. He wasn't ready to complicate his life with any serious commitment.

Steeling himself for the chill in his bedroom, because his landlord was convinced that no one with any degree of intelligence arose at 6.10 am, Paul threw off the blankets and sprinted for the bathroom. Heat was just beginning to clang in the radiators.

By 6.40 am, he was behind the wheel of his car, chosen for low fuel consumption and its ability to fit into the smallest of parking spaces. It took exactly six minutes to drive from his garden apartment complex to the hospital parking lot.

At the hospital Paul went directly up to Pediatrics, stopped at the nurses' station to check with the nurse on duty before he went up to the cafeteria. He was anxious about the little Donovan girl. She had been in and out of the hospital for surgery since she was four. At nine she was philosophical. She was here for tests. Paul prayed no more surgery would be indicated.

The nurse was engrossed in a front page story of the morning newspaper.

"What kind of a night did my girlfriend Donnie spend?" he asked.

"Not bad," the nurse reported, reaching for a chart to give him. "She'll feel lots better after she's seen you. What is it about you, Paulie?" she clucked. "From four to eighty they fall for your bedside manner."

"I took a course," he laughed, skimming the chart. Relieved that nothing new had surfaced.

"Still no word on that little boy who was snatched Sunday night," the nurse reported sorrowfully.

"Maybe he just ran away from home." An aide paused to join the conversation. "Like that fourteen-year-old girl a couple of months ago who was missing for a whole weekend. The cops found her at a girl-friend's house. She was scared to go home when she realized she'd been out till almost half-past three Saturday morning."

"Not this time." The nurse was emphatic. "He was snatched exactly twenty-eight days after the last one. He won't show up, either."

"Isn't it weird?" The aide looked fearful. "I'm sure glad I don't have kids."

"I don't even like going out after dark," the nurse admitted. "And I'm too old to be snatched. The oldest so far was nine."

Paul returned the chart. "I'll be up in the cafeteria for the next twenty minutes. In case my fan club calls."

Waiting in line for a stack of pancakes, Paul read the latest on the Tyrone Randolph case over the shoulder of the intern ahead of him. He felt a personal involvement, like many of the hospital doctors and nurses. Laurie Roberts had rushed down from New York because a friend's nephew was a victim. He didn't really believe she was down here just on business.

He felt a nagging compulsion to become part of stamping out this massacre. He knew about the volunteer groups who went out searching remote areas every weekend. Every time he treated a child in the clinic, he asked himself if this small patient would be the next victim. London had Jack the Ripper. Aurelia, Alabama had the Twenty-Eight Day Monster.

Chapter Nine

Laurie sat in the modest, immaculately clean apartment and listened while a bereaved mother, a toddler clutched to her breast, talked about her dead child.

"I keep tellin' myself, it's God's will," she said in her soft Southern speech. "I keep rememberin' how, when they found my baby, she was wearin' a freshly washed and ironed dress. Somethin' real pretty. Not the jeans and sweater she had on when she went out to play that afternoon." Her voice broke. "I tell myself God didn't let her suffer."

"I'm sure He didn't," Laurie consoled. Not sure at all.

"When are they goin' to find who's killin' our kids?" A note of hysteria crept into the woman's voice. Ted reached over to cover her hand with his in comfort. "How many more will die like my baby?"

"The police are doing everything possible," Ted said. "It's going to stop, Marietta."

"How's Angie?"

"Not good," Ted admitted. "She blames herself for letting Tyrone play in front of the house. But there were a dozen other kids – older than he – out there at the same time," he said in recurrent frustration.

"I still don't know how anybody could have spirited him away."

"Somebody real sick in the head." Marietta pulled the toddler on her lap into a tighter grip. "Somebody that got let out of a hospital when they should have been kept there." Her eyes glowed with fresh rage. "Comin' out onto the streets and murderin' our kids." She turned to focus on Laurie. "You think it'll help if you write that story about the children for that New York magazine?"

"The whole country mourns with you," Laurie said softly. "They know it could happen to any of them. Maybe they'll be more watchful of their own children . . ." But that didn't bring Marietta's daughter back to life.

"Thank you for talking with my friend from New York." Ted rose to his feet, signaling the interview was over.

"You hear anything about Tyrone, you let me know . . ." Marietta rocked gently back and forth with the child in her arms. She didn't expect Tyrone to return alive. Not one of the sixteen other kids had returned alive.

"I'll let you know," Ted promised.

Outside in the cold, damp air again Ted turned to Laurie. "Did you get anything from the interview?" His face was troubled.

"No," Laurie acknowledged. "Did you?"

"Just more frustration. I feel so damn helpless," Ted replied.

"I hated asking all those questions. But I'd hoped some tiny thread would emerge."

"You'll write one hell of a story," Ted surmised. "Jim's going to be amazed."

"Ted, I didn't come down here for a hell of a story." It sounded heartless to talk about an article for the magazine when Tyrone was still missing. "I used that as an excuse to come down to Aurelia. I want to help find Tyrone. To help catch the kidnapper." Somehow, to say 'kidnapper' was less painful than to say 'killer'.

"Get that list from your doctor friend," Ted urged again. "That's helping."

Ted took Laurie on to her next interview, and then to a third. The last interview was with a mother whose nine-year-old son had been missing for three months.

"Nobody has to tell me," she said with fatalistic calm, and Laurie shivered. This mother was working on instinct. "My boy's dead. I thank God I got my five other kids, but life won't ever be right again when one of them is gone. He was such a good boy. Never did no harm. Always polite and sweet. He was an altar boy for almost a year," she said with pride. "We're family folks around here. Church-going, minding our own business. Miss Laurie, who's killing out kids?"

"We'll find out," Laurie vowed. How did she have the gall to make such a statement? The entire Aurelia police force, all those detectives brought in from other parts of the country, the male psychic had not been able to discover the killers.

"You just sit there a few minutes, and I'll bring you some hot chocolate and cookies. It's a nasty, cold day to be running around. Ted, you make sure she don't get her feet wet."

"She's going over to the shoe store to buy a pair of boots before we go anywhere else," Ted reassured with a faint smile. "Don't you worry about that."

"It's bad for Angie, with them having only the one," this mother commiserated. "I praise the Lord every night for my five other kids. But that's not saying I'm not scared for them, too. Nobody goes out once the sun starts going down these days. Not the children, not the grown-ups. We're all scared if we even hear footsteps behind when we're out in the hall."

Laurie and Ted remained to have hot chocolate and cookies, talking in subconsciously hushed tones about Tyrone's disappearance.

"Seems like with all these folks looking for all these months, they'd come up with something. You tell Angie to keep her spirits up. Tyrone's been gone only a couple of days. Maybe he just wandered away and got lost. Maybe he wasn't kidnapped at all."

At last Laurie and Ted were walking out to Angie's car.

"It's depressing," Ted sighed. "I dread going back to the apartment without some encouragement for Angie. Her mother's trying to persuade her to go back to work, but she's too distraught. Even though she works only four hours in the morning – when Tyrone's in school. I'm enraged every time I think of him out there with some lunatic. Scared to death. Wondering what the hell is happening to him."

"Jim okayed an expense account for four days," Laurie said when they were seated in the car. "I'm not going back to New York in four days unless we know Tyrone's all right." She hesitated. "I'll carry the

50

cost myself. This is something I must follow through on, Ted."

"Follow through on dry feet," Ted said with an effort at humour. "I'll drive you over to the shoe store so you can buy a pair of boots."

Ted waited while Laurie debated about which pair of boots to buy. When the decision was made and the clerk went to wrap the boots, Laurie was apologetic. "It's stupid to make such a fuss about which pair of boots to buy when terrible things are happening." Stupid of her to be so anxious that the boots be right for the outfit she planned to wear for her dinner date tonight with Paul Norman. How could she be so drawn to a man she met only yesterday?

"Laurie, the city hasn't stopped living," Ted said. "People go to work, laugh, cry, fight. It's only when the tragedy hits your own family that you feel immobilized."

"I have to be back at the motel by about five," Laurie reminded Ted. Paul would pick her up at six. She needed an hour to revive herself and dress.

Ted consulted his watch.

"It's early. Let's stop by the apartment before I drive you back downtown," Ted said. "I'd like you to meet Angie. She'll be there – she won't leave the phone for a minute. I'll just introduce you as my friend from college who's working on the magazine with me."

"Of course," Laurie agreed.

When they arrived at the door to the Randolph apartment, they heard a woman sobbing inside.

"Angie." Ted was upset. He pushed the doorbell with unconscious intensity.

51

A neighbour admitted them to the apartment. A slender, pretty young woman rocked back and forth in an armchair by the phone. Angie, Laurie realized without introduction. An older woman, whose features were remarkably similar to Angie's stood behind the chair. Silent and in control except for the tears that rolled down her face. Angie's mother. Another neighbour came in from the kitchen with a percolator of coffee in tow. Her eyes were reddened and moist.

"What's happened?" Ted demanded in alarm.

"This . . ." Angie held up a tiny red baseball jacket.

"Somebody found it in the woods down the road," the neighbour who had admitted them into the apartment explained. "It's got Tyrone's name tag sewed in the collar."

"I sewed it into the jacket," his grandmother said, "because so many of the children wore the same kind. But because the jacket showed up doesn't mean something bad has happened to Tyrone." She struggled not to give way to the alarm that assaulted her daughter.

Laurie started at the sound of the doorbell. It was as though everyone in the small but attractively furnished living room expected some ominous news. Ted hurried down the narrow corridor and opened the door.

"It's Bill," he called out. His voice rich with relief.

"I left my house keys here this morning," Bill explained. "I was in a rush. I wanted to stop by the newspaper office on the way to work. I'm running an ad in this evening's newspaper. Offering a reward of five thousand dollars for information that will lead us to Tyrone."

Laurie looked up at Ted's brother-in-law as he

walked into the living room. A clean-cut, slim man in his early thirties with dark eyes that telegraphed his torment.

"Bill, that's the money you were saving towards a down payment on the house," Angie's mother gasped.

"That house won't mean a damn without Tyrone," Bill said tersely.

"Bill, isn't there a substantial reward already being offered by a merchants' group?" Ted asked gently.

"That's different," Bill pinpointed. "The police are handling that. Some people might be afraid to become involved. But they know parents are desperate. Angie and I won't ask questions. We're looking for information that'll bring Tyrone back to us." Bill had become aware of her presence as he talked. Laurie felt uncomfortable beneath his scrutiny.

"Bill, this is Laurie Roberts, my friend from New York," Ted introduced her. "We were at college together. Now she's at the magazine with me. She's writing an article about all this horror for the—"

"What's the matter with you, Ted?" Bill lashed at him. "Isn't it enough we have to endure this kind of agony? Do you have to spread it out for the whole country to wallow in?"

"Bill, everybody is anxious about what's happening down here," Ted began, but Laurie intervened.

"I didn't come to Aurelia because of the article, Bill. I came here because I want to help," Laurie said passionately. "My husband died to save a classroom of children from a terrorist. *I know how you feel.* I'm not here to capitalize on your anguish."

"How do you expect to help?" Bill challenged.

Ted shot Laurie a signal to be silent.

"We'll discuss that later, Bill," he told his brother-in-law.

The two neighbours understood that Ted wished for privacy to talk with Bill. Simultaneously they said their farewells and left.

"All right, Ted. What have you got to tell me?" Bill asked when the two women had left the apartment.

"A theory that Laurie feels strongly about," Ted began and Bill grunted in irritation. "Laurie suspects that Tyrone – and the other children – may have been taken away by some woman who's been deprived of her own child. She's—"

"Ted, sixteen kids have been kidnapped! That's not some deranged mother pining for her child. Six of them have been murdered!"

"Bill, it could be some disturbed woman who takes each child with the hope of replacing a lost child of her own," Laurie insisted. Angie and her mother were listening with an intensity that tightened Laurie's throat. "And then – after a while," she emphasized because Tyrone had been gone less than forty-eight hours, "somebody – her husband or a man friend – for some sick reason takes the child away from her."

The room was heavy with the conjectures that gripped everyone in the room. A man who took away the children – *and murdered them*?

"You hear about women who've lost a baby of their own and then go steal a child." Angie's mother punctured the silence. "It could be happening that way."

"Which leads us where?" Bill's eyes held Laurie's.

"All the children have been kidnapped in this vicinity," Laurie pointed out. "The woman must live around here. Maybe in this area. If we can acquire a list of every child who died within ninety days of the time preceding the first kidnapping, we'll have something to go on."

"Who's handing us over information like that?" Bill was sceptical. He shook his head. "No. It couldn't be that way. A woman might steal one child. But sixteen? One was nine years old! How could she physically get away with it?"

"Bill, it's possible," his mother-in-law insisted. She was a strong woman, yet Laurie sensed her control was fragile now. "We can't overlook any chance. No matter how slight."

"I met a doctor on the plane coming down last night," Laurie told them. "He's a pediatrics resident at Aurelia Hospital. I'm having dinner with him tonight. He's deeply concerned. I'm sure he'll help us."

"Laurie . . ." All at once Angie was calm. "You go ahead. You do whatever you think is right. You find that woman who might have taken Tyrone."

Chapter Ten

The dilapidated old farmhouse, one end of its porch sagging almost to the ground, sat two hundred feet back from a dirt road that was lightly travelled. A clothes line across the porch was weighed down by a pair of quilts left out to air. Situated eighteen miles beyond the city limits, the house was isolated from its neighbours by an expanse of red clay acreage that had gone fallow. The lack of telephone poles and TV aerial lent it an air of belonging to another century, which in truth it did.

In the creeping dusk a hound dog, dozing in the propped-up barn, darted out in sudden frenzy when a small animal bounded across boughs brought down by an electrical storm many weeks earlier but never removed.

In the attic of the farmhouse a lamp glowed beside a cot on which lay a small sleeping boy. At the window hung a heavy, thick black cloth that concealed the illumination from anyone who might drive up to the house, and gaze indoors.

Snow covered the tracks of the Harley that had zoomed up in the early hours of the morning. The woman smoothed the black cloth over the window again. Gus was still sleeping off the beers. He didn't know about this room up in the attic. Nobody knew about it except her.

She deliberately hadn't told Gus about this room when he decided they should move out to the farm she'd inherited when Mama died. He never came up here. He thought it was just storage space where she kept extra quilts and clothes she wasn't ready to throw away yet.

She liked the farm. It was far away from everybody, except for family buried out behind the house. Mama's grave, still so fresh, and Papa's and Granpa's, and all the others. And her precious child, killed in that crash all the way up in South Carolina. Her precious little angel.

When she wanted to go into town – which Gus kept sayin' she wasn't to do – she had Mama's beat-up old 1963 Valiant. It still ran. Sometimes she had to go into town. When the rememberin' got too bad. Gus didn't have to know.

This room was where she used to run to, when she was a little girl and they lived here on the farm. Whenever Mama was mad at her, or when somethin' went wrong and she didn't know how to handle it, she came here. A wisp of a smile touched her doll-like face, so incongruous with the heavy body. This was her special place that nobody knew about.

She walked to the cot and sat in the cane-back chair beside it. She shifted her weight in awareness of the fragility of the chair. Her face softened as she looked at the small boy sleeping on the cot. Her darlin'. Her baby.

She reached out to fondle his head. Nothing bad was gonna happen to this one. She wouldn't let it. Yet terror seeped into her being. She wouldn't lose this one, too. She'd be good. Real good. Only sometimes everythin' got so mixed up in her head.

"Mommie," the little boy mumbled in his sleep. "Mommie . . ." A trace of alarm in his voice now that alerted her to his coming wakefulness.

Lottie reached for the hypodermic syringe in readiness beside the bed. Gus made her quit her job as a practical nurse at the hospital, but she still had her contacts. They knew she wasn't well. They gave her what she needed.

She reached for the small arm and pricked the skin. He'd sleep now. She laid aside the syringe and caressed the appealing little face. She had been expectin' Gus since yesterday mornin'. Now he was home, but he'd stay just a couple of days. He was goin' off on that long haul to California. Then she'd wake up her little boy. They'd have such a good time together. Just the two of 'em.

A sound downstairs, that might just be the wind in the chimney, made her uneasy. She rose to her feet, crossed to the door, peered below. Nothin' to worry about – everythin' was quiet. Gus wouldn't wake up till dark. It was always like that when he returned from a long trip.

She dropped her heavy bulk into the chair, reached to pull the small form into her arms. She nestled his face against her pendulous breast. A radiance shone from her.

She crooned in a voice that could hardly be heard three yards away:

"Sweetes' lil feller—
Everybody knows;
Dunno what ter call 'im,
But he mighty lak' a rose—"

Chapter Eleven

Ted pulled up before the motel and reached over to open the car door for Laurie.

"I'll phone you later to see how you made out with the doctor," Ted said. "That's better than your calling the apartment. Every phone call is traumatic for Angie."

"I know," Laurie commiserated. "If I'm not back then, keep phoning."

In the lobby Laurie hesitated, then headed for the restaurant. She'd pick up a container of tea to take up to her room. She was chilled through. Exhausted from the tension of the last thirty hours.

In her room Laurie kicked off her shoes and settled herself on the bed. The container of tea on the night table beside her. With unsteady hands she managed to remove the top of the container, dropped in the tea bag. She glanced at the clock. Paul would pick her up in an hour and ten minutes.

The hours since Paul Norman had deposited her here at the motel seemed jammed with activity. Yet what had been accomplished? All at once she felt so helpless. Ted had said that while he drove her here. She visualized the photographs of Tyrone that sat on a table in the

Randolph living room. Tyrone as an infant. At three and four and six. Tyrone at his sixth birthday party. Would he see his seventh?

Laurie decided to soak in a bath instead of showering. Her shoulders ached from tension. Now she felt self-conscious about having dinner with a man she met on a plane last night. But two hours with Paul Norman had made her feel as though she had known him for months.

Sipping her tea with a moment of pleasure, enjoying the sybaritic warmth of her room, Laurie allowed her mind to dwell on the three interviews today. Later – before she went to sleep – she would write out notes in longhand. She must not forget that Jim Turner was expecting her to bring in a gripping story.

Angie and Bill could have been living in another neighbourhood in Aurelia, or another town. If they had lived elsewhere, Tyrone might be asleep in his own bed tonight.

With the bath filling, Laurie pulled together her attire for the evening. Glad she had brought along the lilac silk blouse and matching velvet skirt. Festive enough, with a strand of pearls, for wherever Paul would take her for dinner. He was a resident; he would not be overly affluent.

She lowered herself into the soothing warm water. She had left the bathroom door open to hear the classical music she had finally located on a local radio station. Beethoven's *Eroica* was building to a dramatic crescendo.

The phone rang with jarring insistence. Scooping up

a towel to wrap around herself, she hurried out to pick up the phone.

"Hello . . ."

"How are you doing, Laurie?" Jim Turner's voice was crisply enquiring.

"I've had some interviews." She tried to sound enthusiastic. "I may have to stay beyond Friday—"

"Stay." Jim surprised her with his calm acceptance of an extension. "Ask Ted to help you round up a photographer. We'll want lots of pictures. Any indication of a breakthrough?"

"Not yet," Laurie told him. "Ted's brother-in-law has just put up a reward of five thousand for information leading to his little boy. That's on top of the hundred thousand the city merchants are offering. We're all praying something will come through."

"Keep in touch, Laurie. You do a good job on this one, you'll have other assignments."

"Thanks, Jim." Jim didn't know how much more than an assignment this case meant to her.

She dressed slowly. Willing herself to relax. Knowing she had sufficient time. At ten minutes to six Paul called to explain that he'd be about half an hour late.

"I'm tied up here at the hospital," he apologized. "An old tale for a lowly resident. But I won't be later than 6.20 pm," he promised.

"I know hospitals don't run by a clock." Laurie was sympathetic. "Call when you arrive. I'll come right down."

At 6.18 pm Paul phoned up from the lobby. Laurie hurried downstairs. She was startled by her eagerness

63

to see him again. She had been sure she could never feel this way about another man.

Paul was waiting by the elevators. His hair was rumpled. He looked tired.

"I'm sorry I couldn't be on time." His smile was wry. "Occupational hazard."

"No problem," she reiterated.

"I hope you're hungry," he said, a hand at her elbow. "We're having dinner where they cater to those with man-sized appetites."

"I'm starving," she said, laughing lightly. Ted and she had stopped for lunch, which they had barely touched. In the afternoon they'd had hot chocolate and cookies at the apartment where she interviewed a mother. All at once dinner seemed most appealing.

"How long will you be in Aurelia?" Paul asked with disconcerting urgency when they were settled in the car.

"I don't know." The prospect of returning to New York was unsettling.

"You can't be through with the business that brought you down here for at least a week," he said hopefully. "After all, I have to have a chance to get to know you." Laurie was warmed by his candid admiration.

She hesitated. She had not meant to tell him her reasons for being here until further along in the evening. He was curious, though.

"I'm here on an assignment for *Manhattan Weekly*," she said impulsively. That wasn't a lie.

"A story on the kidnappings and murders?" She saw his surge of interest.

"Yes. I sold my publisher on the article because I was anxious to come down here."

"A sort of vacation?"

"No," she denied. "I told you on the plane about a co-worker and friend's nephew being the latest kidnap victim. But even before Tyrone was kidnapped, I wanted to come to Aurelia. I know it sounds insane, but I have such a strong instinct about what's happening."

"Have you talked with the police?" Paul was sympathetic but puzzled.

"No. They'd be sure I was out of my mind."

"Tell me," Paul urged. His eyes deserted the road to rest on her as they stopped for a red light. "I won't think you're out of your mind."

"I know it's a long shot, but it plagues me. You know how the kidnappings occur every twenty-eight days?" Laurie was fighting against discomfort. If Paul laughed at her, she'd be upset. No, she'd be furious. "It's as though somebody was marking the dates on a calendar."

"Go on, Laurie," Paul said quietly.

"It's always a child that's taken. Not specifically girls or boys. A child. I have this eerie conviction that some desperate, lonely woman who's lost a child of her own is kidnapping these children. Each month when she realizes she's not pregnant – not carrying a child – she goes out and kidnaps one. She's a mentally disturbed woman whose child has died recently. Perhaps a few months before the first kidnappings."

"That's not a wild idea." Paul was serious. "That's a strong motive for a woman in that condition. Have you talked with anybody about this?"

"Ted – my friend from the magazine – and his sister and her husband. The police would add it to their list of way-out possibilities. I don't want to see this sitting somewhere on a back burner. I have this strong conviction that if we can trace that woman, we'll find Tyrone. We'll stop more tragedies."

"You figure on checking on children who've died in this section of the city in that time slot," he interpreted. "And tracking down the mothers—"

"That's right." Her heart was pounding. "Paul, can you help us? Your hospital is the one where a child from the local area would have been taken if he was injured or seriously ill."

"It'll take some doing," he warned.

"Will you?" she challenged.

"You bet I will," he told her and grinned. "And all the time I thought it was my boyish charm that made you accept my dinner invitation."

"I wasn't thinking of this when you asked me out." Colour rose along the ridges of her high cheekbones. "I came here with no real plan in mind. But this morning, while Ted and I had breakfast in my motel restaurant, I realized you could be a tremendous help."

"I'll do anything possible to help find that little boy. To stop this massacre." All raillery had vanished. Paul radiated an air of dedication. "But it'll take time."

"We don't have time!" Her eyes pleaded with him to cope with this urgency. "We pray Tyrone's all right. But for how long will he be all right?"

"I'll try to get names and addresses tomorrow. As soon as the chart room opens for the day," Paul said with no hesitation. "When I have it, I'll leave a message at the motel for you to call me. We won't waste a moment."

"Paul, that'll be wonderful." Relief suffused her.

"Don't be hurt if the list of the children who've died in that period leads nowhere," he cautioned. "You said yourself, it's a long shot."

"I know." Intellectually she knew. Emotionally she was convinced this was the right track to lead them to the killers. To Tyrone.

"The restaurant's just ahead." He slowed down for a turn-off. "Do you like *duck á l'orange*?"

"I love it." Her smile was brilliant. She was glad she met Paul Norman on that Delta flight out of LaGuardia. She was glad she was having dinner with him tonight.

"A green salad with blue cheese dressing?"

"What else?" Laurie accepted Paul's lead into a lighter mood. How warm and tender and charming he was. "I knew you were a man who preferred blue cheese dressing."

"And for dessert you can have your choice between Black Forest gateau and peppermint mousse."

"Paul, that's sinful. How will I ever make a choice?"

"You order one and I'll order the other. We'll split. Oh, I have a better idea." His voice was gently teasing. "We'll have Black Forest gateau tonight. Tomorrow night we'll have the peppermint mousse."

"How can I refuse an offer like that?" He meant to see much of her while she was here, her mind registered with pleasure.

But over dinner, despite their silent pact to make this a festive evening, they were inexorably drawn

67

into fresh discussion of the nightmare that blanketed Aurelia.

"Paul, we will find Tyrone in time. Won't we?" she pleaded for reassurance.

"Laurie, we'll do our damnedest."

Chapter Twelve

Laurie and Paul lingered over dinner as long as was decently possible. She had told him about Mark and was warmed by his compassion.

"I should have arranged for tickets for a concert or a play," he said ruefully. She sensed he was reluctant – as she was – to end the evening this early. "Look, why don't you come with me to the hospital while I pop in to visit a salty great-grandmother who's recovering from a lateral bypass on one leg. She's been worrying since we first met two weeks ago that I have no time for a social life. You'll bail me out."

"I'd love to meet a salty great-grandmother who's just had a lateral bypass," she said, laughing.

"You'll like Peggy," he promised. "She's a delight. Not my patient," he emphasized. "A friend. We met when she came up to Pediatrics the night before her surgery. She was visiting a neighbour's grandchild."

She would be down here for a short while, Laurie reminded herself while they drove to the hospital. It wasn't as though something serious would develop between Paul and her. Yet she knew that the emotional involvement between them was far beyond what was normal for a twenty-four hour acquaintanceship.

They parked and walked towards the sprawling, modern hospital complex. Paul's hand at her elbow. There was no need for protection in this brightly lit area. Paul was eager for this slight physical contact. He wouldn't make a pass, would he? For an instant she was uncomfortable. No. Paul was too sensitive. He knew she was still hurting from Mark's death.

"We'll go up to Four so I can check out a patient, then we'll visit with Peggy for a few minutes. After that I'll show you our cafeteria. By this time of night the coffee's vile. We'll have tea." Meaning, they could sit in the cafeteria and talk. No pass, she recognized with relief.

Laurie was conscious of the interested scrutinies on the part of the nurses on duty on the Fourth Floor. She guessed that Paul did not make a habit of bringing his dates into the hospital. She waited by the nurses' station while Paul looked in on a patient. He returned to collect her, and they took the elevator up three floors.

White-haired and still a good-looking woman in her late seventies, Peggy was propped up against a pair of pillows and listening intently to a radio newscaster. On the table beside the bed were half a dozen mystery titles from the hospital library wagon and the current issue of *Cosmopolitan*.

"If you're busy, we'll come back later," Paul teased from the doorway.

"If you leave before I've a chance to talk to that gorgeous dish beside you, I'll put arsenic in your coffee." Peggy's smile was ingratiating. "Come sit down here," she invited Laurie and patted one side of the bed.

70

"This is Laurie Roberts. Peggy Lane," Paul introduced them. "I warn you, Laurie. She's got a tongue that'll put a New York dockhand to shame when she's riled. And she'll charm you into believing she's a darling little old lady with nothing more evil in her mind than knitting for the church bazaar."

"I'm already charmed," Laurie said.

"You're from New York," Peggy pounced with triumph in her magnolia-velvet voice.

"That's right," Laurie admitted.

Peggy squinted in thought. "You a newspaper reporter? Down here to write a story about those terrible murders?"

"I work for a magazine," Laurie acknowledged.

"She's written paperback mysteries," Paul added with a wink at Laurie.

"One mystery." Laurie was determined to brush aside the glamour Paul tried to infer. "For which I received a total of two thousand dollars. I can't make a living writing mysteries. Not yet."

"So the magazine sent you down to do an article about those poor little kids?" Peggy asked.

"That's my assignment." Laurie was grave.

"What do you think about these murders?" Peggy was avid for her opinion.

"Tell her, Laurie," Paul urged.

Laurie explained her suspicions. Peggy listened, absorbing every word.

"I'll bet you grew up on Agatha Christie." Peggy flashed an elfin grin.

"Do you think I'm just plotting a mystery?" Laurie was uneasy.

"No." Peggy was decisive. "I think you have a woman's instinct working together with a mystery writer's mind. That's a powerful combination. Look, if they can listen to psychics, why not you?"

"Because it's too much of a long shot," Laurie pointed out.

"I learned a long time ago that there are times in life when only a long shot pays off. You two doing something about this?" Her eyes moved from Laurie to Paul.

"We're trying." Paul was serious now. "The little boy that disappeared night before last is the nephew of a friend of Laurie's."

"That puts the ball in your court." Peggy nodded. "Where do you go from here?"

"*Cherchez la femme*," Paul said. "Find a mother who lost her child just before the kidnappings began."

"You think it was a child who died here in this hospital?" Peggy pursued.

"We're praying it is." Now Paul seemed apprehensive.

"Cover your bets." Peggy was brisk. "Check every hospital in the county. Not just this one. You can get a team together," she pushed ahead because Paul was about to protest. "The police can't follow every wild lead. This is your ball game. Call my old man. Frank'll pitch in. He knows everybody within a hundred and fifty mile radius of Aurelia. He's an ex-police officer. Six foot three and gentle as a kitten, but nobody knows that but me." She chuckled. "Sometimes I tell him I robbed the cradle when I married him — he's fourteen years younger than me. But we've been married seven years, and we figure it's working great."

She reached into a drawer of the night table beside her bed. "Here's our phone number at home. Frank's come and gone for the night. They've got this damn rule here at the hospital that he has to leave at eight o'clock. If they had any feelings for patients, they'd install double beds for those that are married and let mates have sleep-in privileges," she grumbled. "Aha, I shocked you." She laughed at Laurie's unwary astonishment. "We may be getting on a bit, but we haven't forgotten what it's like to be young and in love." Now she focused on Paul. "Remember, call Frank first thing tomorrow morning."

"Was I wrong about Peggy?" Paul asked Laurie while he piloted her into the large, white-walled cafeteria, where only a sprinkling of hospital personnel occupied tables at this hour.

"I love her." Laurie felt a surge of affection for Peggy Lane. "She meant it, didn't she? About our calling her husband to help?"

"Oh, sure." Again they both relinquished banter. "But Peggy's right. It would be naïve for us to think we can nail the woman we want by going through the files of just this hospital. If we're lucky, we will – but we can't count on it. I'll call Frank in the morning."

"It's frightening to think how much ground we have to cover. But like Peggy said, the police can't follow every wild lead."

"Your friend Ted and his brother-in-law are on the

team," Paul reminded. "Now we have Frank Lane. I know a pair of doctors at County General. I'll call them and tell them what we need, then send Frank over there to stir them into action. Ted, Bill, and you can tackle the lists we draw in. We have to move fast. We're pretty sure there won't be another kidnapping for three weeks." He paused, seemed almost apologetic. "We don't know how long Tyrone has—"

"Paul, what are the police doing?" Frustration made her sharp.

"Not one cop in the area has had a day off for months," Paul admonished gently. "They've made house-to-house searches from one end of the city to the other. They're out with dogs trained for police work."

"Maybe Tyrone isn't in the city." This supposition was unsettling.

"The police force has just so much manpower. Believe me, they're doing everything possible." He reached a hand across the table to cover hers.

"I'm scared," Laurie confessed. "Poor little Tyrone. Poor Angie. Poor Bill."

"I'll go after those names tomorrow as fast as I can. Maybe Frank can talk to the Pediatric Services on other hospitals in the fringe areas. He'll know the gimmicks to dig out information. Like Peggy said, let's don't overlook anything."

"As soon as you have the list, you'll leave word at the motel switchboard for me?"

"Right." Paul nodded. "And remember, we're having dinner tomorrow night. We have a date with a pair of peppermint mousses."

"Something useful will surface tomorrow." Laurie's optimism was belied by the anxiety in her eyes.

"I'll take you back to the motel," Paul said when she reached a hand to her mouth to stifle a yawn. "You're beat, and I'm due at the hospital at seven am."

Chapter Thirteen

While she turned the key in the lock of her door, Laurie looked at her watch. It was almost eleven! Ted must have been trying to reach her. It was unbelievable, the way the hours had raced past in Paul's company.

She pulled off her boots, changed into nightie and robe. She felt a surge of guilt that it was so late. She couldn't call Angie's apartment at this hour. Not at any hour – unless it was with good news.

Impatient to dispel the silence, she switched on the television. The eleven pm news invaded the room. She stood immobile at the brief report on Tyrone's disappearance, the painful recap of the repeated disappearances of the children of Aurelia. Tyrone had been missing over forty-eight hours. *They were running our of time.*

The phone rang. Laurie darted to pick up the receiver.

"Hello." She dropped to the edge of the bed.

"I've been trying to reach you since nine," Ted began.

"I'm sorry!" she said apologetically. "Paul and I sat over half a dozen cups of tea and looked for angles."

"You know that personal reward Bill put up yesterday?" Ted's voice ricocheted with excitement. "We've had an answer. An elderly man. He sounds scared to death, but he's willing to meet us at a roadside diner about four miles out of town. Tomorrow morning at seven."

"Couldn't you see him tonight?"

"He said he can't drive in the dark. Some visual problem. He won't let us come to his place. I'm going with Bill to meet him. You want to come along?"

"Sure," Laurie agreed instantly. "If you think that won't scare him off."

"You sit at a table nearby. He won't know you're there. I'll try to manage that he's facing you. You might pick up something that Bill and I miss. He could be a nut, but we can't overlook any possibility."

"When do we see your psychologist friend?" Laurie asked.

"We'll have lunch together at noon tomorrow." Ted seemed to be drained of breath. "What developed with your pediatrics resident?"

Laurie briefed him on Paul's belief that they should check on hospitals in the outlying areas. She told him about Frank Lane being drafted for their team. Ted agreed that pinning their hopes on one hospital was shaky.

"I'm not sure what we'll do when we have those names," he admitted. "We're clutching at straws."

"We'll divide up the names and locate the families." Her mind was rushing into action. "We'll say we're doing a survey on the ages of the children in the neighbourhood. For an article on the Aurelia kidnappings," she improvised. "A disturbed woman won't be that hard to spot if we start asking questions."

"I'm not sure this is legal." Ted was uneasy.

"I'm researching the story for *Manhattan Weekly*. Bill and you are helping me. The article is legitimate. And we're not interfering with the police."

"What kind of questions should we ask? What do we look for?" Ted was disconcerted by the task ahead.

"Your psychologist friend will tell us that. When we run into a strong lead, we can go to the police. But we have to move fast." Anxiety tugged at her.

"I know," Ted said tersely. "I keep thinking, *every hour* is crucial. I wish to hell we could work around the clock."

"The police are doing that," Laurie reminded. "Maybe they'll find Tyrone before we do." But she didn't believe that. They had not found one of the sixteen other children who had disappeared. Only six bodies.

"Laurie, Bill and Angie are grateful for your help."

"I hope we give them real reason to be grateful." Was it wrong to build Angie and Bill's hopes on her instinct? "About tomorrow, Ted. Shall I arrange for a car rental?" She had not driven in almost two years. Not since she had moved to New York from the Boston suburb.

"I'll drive you over to the apartments' parking area. You can take Angie's car. I'll pick you up in the morning at 6.30am. That'll give us time to make the appointment at the diner."

Despite her exhaustion Laurie lay back against the pillows and stared into the darkness. Her mind was too stimulated to allow her to sleep. She tried one position after another. Tried meditation. Every effort was futile.

At 12.30am she threw aside the covers, switched on

her bedside lamp, and crossed to her suitcase to pull out one of the yellow legal pads she had brought along for note taking. She should have taken notes during her interviews with the three mothers. Yet she sensed they would be less constricted if she seemed only to listen.

She had not even brought her tape recorder to the interviews. Some people froze once the tape recorder switch was flipped. The urgency in tracking down Tyrone made the article she was here to write seem unreal.

Again she asked herself if she was wrong to give Angie and Bill hopes based on instinct. But so many times in her life instinct had been right. When her car broke down that day two years ago, she had sensed that something was wrong. That she ought to be with Mark.

Now she dug out a cluster of pens and returned to the bed. With the pillows propped against the headboard she began to make notes. Hoping something would connect and lead the way to Tyrone.

Instinct kept insisting a disturbed woman, aware every twenty-eight days that she did not carry a child, went berserk and sought a stranger's child to claim secretly as her own. Six of the children had been murdered. *Not by the woman*, she was sure. But find the woman, and they'd find the murderer.

Chapter Fourteen

Gus turned over on his back beneath the pile of patchwork quilts that covered the sagging old bedstead. He reached out an arm for Lottie. She had stuffed him with so much supper he'd been too tired for anything except sleep when they got into bed.

He remembered Lottie snuggling up against him just before he fell off into more of those crazy dreams. All Lottie wanted to do when he was home was to make love. She cried when he reminded her that the doctor up in South Carolina – where the accident had happened – said it wouldn't be good for her to get pregnant. Not until her head was better.

All at once he was fully awake. Alarmed. Where the hell was Lottie? *She swore she wouldn't do it again.*

He threw off the covers and stumbled in the dark cold to the hallway. The night light was on in the hall. Lottie was scared of the dark. Especially when she was here in the house by herself. Didn't she know that suspicious old hound dog would scare away anybody that tried to get in?

"Lottie?" he yelled. "What the hell are you doin? It's one o'clock in the mornin'."

He pushed open the door of the bedroom across

81

from their own and fumbled in the dark for a light. His heart was thumping. He remembered all the times he had walked into this room and found some dumb kid drugged on the bed.

There was no kid here tonight. Only the fancy-dressed doll he had bought her in New Orleans. Away on the last trip he had worried every minute. It was that time of the month. Why did he always have to be away from town part of that week? *That's when it happened.* But when he came home last night, he found no kid in the bedroom.

Gus moved to the head of the stairs and bellowed, "Lottie? Where the hell are you?"

"Sugar, what you yellin' about?" Lottie hovered at the top of the rickety stairs that led to the attic, where she liked to store her mama's old patchwork quilts and clothes that ought to be thrown out. With her weight you'd think she'd be scared to death to climb those stairs. He kept warning her about that. "I went up for another quilt. It's so cold in the house when the wind's blowin' the way it is tonight."

"Come back to bed, Lottie. I'll make you warm," he promised. Relief surged through him. When would he stop worrying about her? Each time she promised it wouldn't happen again.

"You want some hot coffee?" Lottie asked solicitously. "I'll bring up a pot. Hot coffee always makes you feel good on cold nights."

"Yeah, you bring up a pot of coffee."

Gus went back into the bedroom and threw a few more chunks of coal into the grate. Now he climbed back into bed, pulled the quilts over him. This house

82

wasn't fit for livin' in, the way the cold kept comin' through the cracks. He hated to waste money insulatin' a beat-up old house like this. Maybe he'd buy a Franklin stove for the bedroom. They threw a lotta heat.

The doctor said the farm would be good for Lottie. She needed a change of scenery. He took the new job so he'd have money to buy her nice things, even though he didn't like bein' away from home half the time. Every time he came back from a trip, he brought Lottie a present. She had a roomful of those fancy dolls he'd bought her.

Maybe if he got rid of the car and she couldn't get to town, that craziness would stop. But he couldn't do that. Suppose she got sick or somethin'? She had to have a car to get to a hospital. They didn't even have a phone out here.

Lottie didn't want a phone. She said they only brought bad news. She had a real fit when he tried to talk to her about puttin' in a phone so he could call her when he was out on the road.

If he took the car keys and hid them, she'd never be able to leave the place. But he was scared she might come down with the flu or somethin' and not be able to get to a doctor. She didn't have to go out for food. Not with the way he kept the freezer loaded up. And that little country store had orders to bring out eggs and milk and bread twice a week. They left it in a box on the back porch, and he paid for them when he got back into town.

Downstairs Lottie was singing as she fixed the coffee. Why was he so crazy about that woman? She had a face like one of those kewpie dolls he won at the county fair when he was a kid. She was his woman. No matter what she did, he had to take care of her.

Despite the coldness in the room he began to sweat. He was remembering the first time she went into that craziness. He had come back from the trip to Cleveland. Before he got on the Harley, he had a few beers with Chuck. He had driven the bike into the barn and hurried towards the house . . .

The moon was a pale circle against the hills in the distance. The old farmhouse, hungry for paint, was bathed in its light. As he stalked towards the house, the dog on the porch woke up. He started to yap.

"Shut up, Clarence," he ordered and the dog charged forward in delirious welcome. "Hey, boy, you take care of Lottie for me?" He wrestled with Clarence for a few minutes, then let himself into the house.

The night light was on in the upstairs hall, the way it always was. Most times Lottie was in bed by nine o'clock. She wouldn't watch television or listen to the radio any more. She wouldn't let him put up a TV aerial so he would watch the sports events without all that interference. But tonight she was awake. He could hear her singin':

> "Sweetes' lil feller—
> Everybody knows;
> Dunno what ter call 'im,
> But—"

"Lottie!" he interrupted in pleased surprise. For once she wasn't sittin' around cryin'. She sounded almost happy. The doctor said it was just a matter of time before she'd be all right, didn't he?

"Gus?" Lottie came out into the hall in her nightgown and bathrobe. "Oh, honey, I'm so glad to see you!"

She came awkwardly down the stairs, that kewpie doll face of hers lookin' like it was Christmas Eve and she knew she had a pile of presents waitin' under the tree.

"Hey, Sugar, that's the way I like to see you look." He swatted her across the rump. *Lottie was all right.*

"You hungry?" Lottie pressed her bulk against his. "I got some stew I could heat up. And some collard greens just needin' a few minutes on the stove."

"That sounds fine, Lottie."

Together they went out into the kitchen. While she fussed with the pots, he threw coal into the small pot-bellied stove that sat at one side of the kitchen and talked to her about the trip. It was like old times. The doctor said that once she got her head together, they could try to make her pregnant again.

Jesus, it had hurt him to see Lottie the way she was these last few weeks. He worried about her every minute he was away. But he had to work. Nobody was puttin' food on the table if he didn't work.

He was proud of makin' out so good, Gus thought. With Lottie all right, they wouldn't have to stay out here on the creepy old farm. With the wages he was gettin' on the long-haul jobs, they could think about buyin' a decent little house for themselves.

All of a sudden, while Lottie spooned the stew into a plate, he heard a child crying upstairs. *In this house?*

"Lottie, who's that?" Without knowing why, he was scared.

"Our son, Gus." Lottie beamed. "I had to tie him onto the bed so he wouldn't fall off."

"What the hell did you do?" He pushed back his chair, rushed from the kitchen and out to the stairs, with Lottie trailing after him.

"Honey, don't you frighten him now. I had him all calmed down, nice and quiet. You be careful, Gus. Don't scare him."

The crying led him into the bedroom opposite their own. He charged inside. A little boy of about five lay huddled beneath a quilt. Lengths of clothes line held him down on the bed.

"Mama, Mama," he sobbed. "I want my Mama . . ."

"Honey, I'm your Mama . . ." Lottie shoved past Gus to go to the little boy on the bed. "You're our precious lil' baby now. We're gonna have such good times together." Lottie dropped to her knees beside the bed and fondled his small head. "He ate two hot dogs for dinner and a load of French fries. He's gonna eat us out of house and home," she said with delight.

"Jesus Christ, Lottie!" Gus exploded. "That's the kid on the front pages of all the newspapers. He's been missin' four days! Every cop in the county is lookin' for him!"

"He's our son now." Lottie's face was bathed in maternal pride. "You be quiet now," she pleaded with the flailing little boy. "Then I can take off the rope. You're gonna be just fine."

"You kidnapped the kid!" Gus was dizzy with disbelief. They could spend the rest of their lives in jail if the cops caught them with the boy. They'd never believe Lottie took him herself. They'd blame him, too.

"Lottie, you know better than to do somethin' like that."
She was still out of her mind. Worse than before. "How
the hell did you do it?"

"It was easy." She clutched the two small hands in
hers while she talked. "I went back to Aurelia. It was
almost dark. Nobody noticed me, by the apartment
block. I'd got ethyl chloride from Myrtle at the hospital.
I told her we got another litter of kittens, and you
wanted me to get rid of them. Just a little of that
sweet-smellin' stuff, and he went right to sleep. He
don't weigh nothin' at all. I put him in the car and
brought him home. He'll get to understand soon that
he belongs to us. He'll stop all this carryin' on."

"Lottie, I gotta take him back."

"No!" Lottie threw herself across the small boy on
the bed. "You can't take him away. You can't! You
killed Junior and the new baby that wasn't even born!
You can't have this one!"

"Lottie, it wasn't my fault that truck was comin'
head-on on the wrong side of the road!" It wasn't
his fault that Junior got killed and Lottie lost the baby
she'd been carrying for five months. Not his fault that
Lottie was out of her head. "I'm gonna take this kid
back where he belongs."

"You can't, Gus! You can't do that!" Lottie fought
with him while he struggled to pull her away from the
bed. "He's my baby! He's my baby!"

Sweating and breathless, he locked her up in their
bedroom, and paused uneasily. Would the hook and
eye hold against her pounding on the door that way?
He'd put the hook and eye on the door to keep Clarence
from pushing his way into the room and jumping up

87

on the bed when he wasn't around. Clarence could sleep anywhere he wanted in this house except on their bed.

"Gus, you can't take my baby! You can't take him away. Not this one!" Lottie pounded on the door with both fists.

What was he gonna do with the kid? He couldn't just walk into the police and say, "look what I found." The kid must be five or six – he'd tell the cops what happened. But Lottie said she got him from an apartment block in Aurelia. He'd take the kid to the lobby and leave him there. Somebody'd take him where he belonged. He'd leave him and clear out fast.

Gus went into the bedroom and untied the child on the bed. Why the hell didn't the little brat shut up?

"You wanna go home?" he demanded.

All at once the little boy was silent. He looked up at Gus with huge, frightened eyes. He nodded convulsively.

"OK, I'll take you home. Just you be quiet," he warned. "Don't you start carryin' on anymore. I'm takin' you home," he repeated, pulling a knife from his back pocket to use in cutting the rope.

He hoisted the trembling frame into his arms and hurried down the stairs and out to the barn. Moonlight lent an eerie brightness to the night. He shifted the boy under one arm while he struggled to open the door. He swore under his breath. The doors were jammed again.

"You stand right here," he exhorted as he put the boy down. "I'll get the car out of the barn, and I'll drive you home. I'll buy you an ice-cream," he cajoled while he tried to manipulate the warped doors.

He froze at the sound of a car coming down the dirt road. Dragging its muffler. Suddenly the little boy made a wild dash for freedom. Heading for the road.

"Hey!" He lunged forward, astonished at how fast a five-year-old in frenzy could run. "You ain't goin' no place!"

He closed in on the fleeing figure, dropped with him behind a clump of bushes.

"Mama! Mama!" The high young voice rose into the night air. "Mama, come get me!"

Gus clamped a hand over the small mouth. A flying foot caught him in the groin. A bellow of pain escaped him. He loosened his hold.

"Mama! Mama!" The anguished cry was startlingly loud in the stillness of the night.

"Shut up," he hissed. The car was coming close. "For Chrissake, shut up!"

His large, powerful hand reached to cover the small mouth. He was unaware, in his panic, that his other hand had closed in about the slender throat. He stared out towards the road in terror until the car passed the house. Its muffler providing a raucous farewell.

Only now did he realize the small body hung limp from his hands. Like the bird he'd pulled from a trap last month.

For a few minutes he squatted there on the dirt. Not knowing what to do. Then he went out to the barn, wrestled with the door, and brought out the old Valiant. He threw the body into the trunk along with a shovel. He'd go out to the spot where he fished every spring. Nobody would ever know what happened . . .

Gus heard Lottie lumbering up the stairs with his coffee. She seemed real happy again just to have him home. He never hit her until he came back from the Memphis haul and found the last kid stashed in the other bedroom. He should have given her a beatin' a long time ago, he told himself. That taught her she had to stop this craziness.

Lottie was OK now. He'd come home this time, and everything was OK. But they'd stay out here, away from folks. Each time the cops dug up another body, he got nervous. But what was the difference if it was one kid he took care of, or sixteen? The cops would put Lottie and him away for the rest of their lives even if it was only the one kid.

He hadn't meant for it to happen that way. He was just tryin' to take care of his woman.

Chapter Fifteen

Normally Paul fell asleep the minute he hit the pillow. Tonight he lay awake, staring at the ceiling of his one bedroom garden apartment. Talking to Laurie on the plane he had sensed she was special. Tonight had confirmed it. Impulsive decisions were not his style. That was why the thoughts about Laurie that ricocheted through his brain were disconcerting.

His socializing since med school had been restricted to gatherings with other doctors and with nurses he met at the hospital. For a while he had seen an attractive pediatrics resident, without becoming seriously involved. He'd always told himself a doctor could make no commitments until he was established in practice.

In September his residency would be finished. He was already in correspondence with an upstate doctor at the edge of retirement, eager to bring in a young doctor who shared his convictions about medicine.

In April he had two weeks leave. He planned on going home, then calling on Dr Collier. The old doctor was pushing eighty and still carrying on. A wonderful guy, Paul thought with respect. The town had given a big dinner for him last year to express their gratitude for his services. He had been their doctor for fifty-two years.

Maybe he could spend a week of his leave in New York. Dad's firm kept a corporate apartment in the city. If Dad put in a bid fast enough, he might get it for a few days. He'd be able to see Laurie in New York. She couldn't be staying down here long if she had a job on a magazine up there.

He was exhausted. He had been awake since before six in the morning. Why the devil didn't he fall asleep? He turned over and burrowed his face in the pillow. In less than five hours his alarm would be going off.

Slowly Paul became aware that his phone was ringing. It took another thirty seconds for him to remember that a phone call in the middle of the night meant a hospital emergency.

He pulled himself over to one side and reached for the phone. Fully awake now.

"Yeah?" Squinting he checked with the clock on his night table. It was 2.05am. "What's the problem?"

As he'd suspected, the call was from the hospital. A fire had swept through a row of flimsy wooden houses. They were swamped with burn and smoke poisoning cases.

"I'll be there in seven or eight minutes."

He reached for his trousers. He visualized the parade of ambulances bringing stretchers into the hospital. They'd be busy straight through to his morning shift. He hoped the car would start up without trouble in this cold.

The antifreeze was doing its job. The car turned over

with no delay. This time of night the roads were empty. Cleared of slush. He arrived at the hospital in record time. To chaos in the emergency room.

It was almost three hours later before the situation was under control. Too late to go back to the apartment, Paul assessed. He would conk out in the doctors' lounge until it was time to go on his shift.

En route to the lounge he changed his direction and headed for the cafeteria. He'd need at least two cups of coffee before he started his rounds. Walking into the cafeteria he visualized Laurie sitting with him over endless cups of tea last night.

Laurie could fit into his life as neatly as though born for that purpose. He didn't have to keep seeing her for six months to know that. Not that he would rush her, he cautioned himself. She had been hurt by Mark's death. But, somehow, he must let her realize this wasn't just a casual interlude.

Paul collected a cup of coffee and took it to a table. Only a sprinkling of hospital personnel sat round the room at this hour.

"Paul!" An emergency room nurse with whom he had been working for the past three hours rushed towards him.

"Not another fire?" he asked in mock panic.

"No. A battered kid was brought in. He was found wandering in the street. They're sending him up to Pediatrics now. I know how involved you've been with that group working with battered children. I thought you'd want to know." She paused. "He's a little boy of about five or six. No ID on him. They've called the police. He might be that missing child."

"Thanks!" Paul left his coffee and rushed from the cafeteria.

En route to Pediatrics he stopped at a public phone, debated for an instant, then reached for a coin. From the information operator he acquired the motel phone number, called Laurie. If the police brought over Tyrone's family for identification, she would want to be here with them.

"Hello . . ." Her voice was hazy with sleep.

"Laurie, it's Paul. This may be nothing at all, but I wanted to tell you—"

"What is it?" She was fully awake.

"An ambulance just brought in a battered child. He has no ID on him, but he's about five or six."

"Paul, is he all right?"

"I haven't seen him yet. But he's alive. We don't know that he's Tyrone," Paul cautioned.

"I'll be over as fast as I can dress and grab a taxi."

Paul went to Pediatrics. As always, every doctor and every nurse on the floor was angry that a child had been mistreated. He went into the room where the tiny figure lay in the high hospital bed. Head bandaged, one eye half-closed, mouth swollen. He moaned incoherently.

"Could you get anything out of him?" Paul asked the intern who leaned over him with obvious compassion.

"Not yet. I'd like to tear the creep to shreds, whoever it was that did this. Nasty gash on the back of the head. A concussion. Bruises all over his body."

For the next few minutes Paul and the intern concentrated on examining their small patient. All hospital personnel were geared to watch for battered children. This was a flagrant case.

"What kind of a human being beats up a kid?" The intern grimaced in disgust.

"He has to be sick," Paul said with frustration. "Or she has to be sick," he expanded. Plenty of times the police tracked down mothers who'd sadistically beaten their children. "Whoever did it belongs in a psychiatric clinic."

Had the detectives checked out hospital psychiatric records in looking for the 'Twenty-Eight Day Killer'? That would be a problem. Psychiatrists were bound to confidentiality. But that could provide a short-cut. Again, he felt a surge of frustration. How many more children would die before the killer was caught?

A child's life was so precious. Each time they lost a child at the hospital he felt a personal loss. He was angry at himself that he had not known enough to stave off death.

As the two doctors turned away from the bed, a pair of detectives appeared at the door with badges in hand.

"Can you recognize him from the snapshot?" one detective asked the other, while he inspected the small battered face with a compassion undiminished by probably twenty years of police service.

"With those injuries I don't know," the second detective admitted.

The two detectives questioned the doctor who had accompanied the little boy from the emergency room, and made notes. While they talked, Paul heard a flurry of footsteps in the hall. Two men appeared.

"I'm Bill Randolph," the shorter man identified himself. His eyes clung to the face of the child on the bed. "No," he said with anguish. "That's not Tyrone."

"Thank God, we didn't tell Angie," the other man said.

"Are you Ted Craig?" Paul asked in sudden comprehension.

"Yes." Ted was astonished that Paul knew him.

"I'm Paul Norman. Laurie's friend," he introduced himself. "I'm not on duty yet. That is, not officially. Why don't we go to the cafeteria for coffee?"

"We have time," Ted said to Bill. "We don't have to pick up Laurie until 6.30am."

"She's coming here," Paul told them, moving them from the room. Before the detectives became curious. "I called her as soon as I heard the boy had been brought in. We'd hoped it was Tyrone."

While they paused at the nurses' station so that Paul could give instructions about the battered child, the elevator door opened. Laurie darted out and walked towards them.

"It wasn't Tyrone," Ted told her and her face lost its aura of hope.

"They didn't want to let me upstairs," Laurie said while they waited for an elevator to take them up to the cafeteria. She turned to Paul. "I told them I was your cousin from Albany and that you'd asked me to meet you for an early breakfast."

"We need to organize our actions." Seeing the pain in Bill Randolph's eyes, Paul had known he was wholly committed to this operation. "I'm calling friends at the other hospitals to solicit help. Let's sit down in the cafeteria and plot out each step we should take. We're a team now."

Chapter Sixteen

Ted and Bill drove Laurie to the apartments' parking area, where they took her to Angie's 1994 Pontiac. Bill gave her the keys. In twenty minutes they were to meet the man who had called in response to the ad offering a reward for information leading to Tyrone.

"You go in ahead of us, Laurie," Bill instructed. "He may be there waiting. We don't want him to connect you with us."

"Does he know Ted's coming with you?" Laurie asked Bill anxiously.

"I said I'd be there with my brother-in-law. He wasn't too happy, but he agreed. I said I'd be wearing a red turtleneck – he can't miss me." Bill tugged at the neck of his sweater. "If you see some old guy at a table alone, go to the table beyond him and sit so you can see his face. Pretend you're reading a magazine. There . . ." He pointed to a copy of a magazine on the front seat of Angie's car.

"Where is the diner?" Laurie was uneasy driving on strange roads when time was a factor. People were pouring out of the apartment buildings now, converging on the parking area. *En route* to jobs. The city was moving into another day.

"Follow us," Bill said. "I'll pull off about a half mile before the diner. Then you can just drive straight ahead. It'll be on that road. A right turn at the Big Chief diner."

Laurie waited for Bill to pull out, then followed. She was nervous about keeping Bill's car in sight. When they swung onto the highway, a truck pulled out in front of her. She leaned over the wheel, determined not to lose Bill and Ted.

Because she was unfamiliar with the road, it seemed that the distance was far longer than indicated on the dashboard mileometer. Then, at last, Bill was pulling off the road. She waved a hand when she passed the car. Was the man Bill was meeting a crackpot? Or would he bring them a genuine lead?

Nobody had come up with information in response to the substantial reward posted by the merchants' group and increased by the city, Laurie recalled. Bill could be right in believing that a reward offered by a parent – no questions asked – might be less intimidating.

Laurie tensed in alertness. A large sign rose into view just ahead. Big Chief. On the right, as Bill had told her. At the turn-off to the diner she left the road and swung into the parking area. Only four cars were here this early in the morning. Plus a truck. The cars, she surmised, belonged to employees.

The morning was brisk and cold, but sunny. The windows of the diner steamed over, attesting to the warmth inside. As Laurie climbed the stairs and opened the door to the diner, she spied Bill's car turning off the road. The clock in the diner, hanging on the wall opposite the door, read 6.55am.

The booth to the far left was occupied by a pair of truck drivers, arguing in high spirits about the merits of a hockey team. One of them was smoking a cigar. That was reason enough for her to seek a booth at the opposite end of the diner.

She went to the booth at the end, sitting at the side that faced the door. She picked up the magazine she had brought with her from the car and pretended to be absorbed in an article. A waitress came over with a menu. While Laurie ordered, Ted and Bill walked inside. They sat in the next booth, their backs to her. Which meant the man they were to meet would be facing her. If he showed.

Ted and Bill appeared involved in a discussion on home insulation. The waitress presented them with menus. While they deliberated, Laurie glanced out the window. A vintage Ford in need of a paint job was moving to the side of the parking area.

In moments the man who had been driving the Ford was at the door of the diner. He was small, slight, in his late seventies, Laurie judged. An ungloved hand held the collar of his overcoat close about his throat. He squinted behind metal-rimmed glasses. Seemingly uneasy at being here.

Laurie saw Bill reach a hand up to his red turtleneck as though in encouragement. Laurie buried her face in the magazine. At the other end of the diner one of the truck drivers dropped money into the jukebox. She gritted her teeth in frustration. Would she be able to hear?

The man opened his frayed overcoat as he walked to the booth where Ted and Bill waited for him. His eyes enquiring. Uncertain.

"You said breakfast at seven?" Ted said in an effort to reassure him, and the timorous little man slid into a seat opposite with a look of relief.

"I ain't sure I ought to be here." He looked from Ted to Bill. "My wife was against it. She said I might be cutting my throat."

"Nobody will hurt you," Bill soothed while Laurie strained to hear. In truth, the music from the jukebox was a protective screen for the conference between the three men. "Just tell us what you know. I'm Tyrone's father. This is his uncle."

The three men fell silent as the waitress approached Laurie's booth with her orange juice. She acknowledged it with a quick smile and returned to perusing the magazine. Ostensibly engrossed in its contents.

With the waitress behind the counter again, the small elderly man resumed the conversation.

"You can't tell nobody where you got this from," the would-be informer stipulated. "He'd be out to get me."

"Nobody will know," Bill promised.

"My wife and me, we spend a lot of time in the house. We got a little place out of town, that's separated from the farm next door by some woods. When it's cold and we can't go out much, we like to sit by the window and look out. We live on Social Security so we ain't got no money to waste. Sometimes we sit by the window without even turning on the lights. To save on the electric bill. Just so long as we have some little light from the fireplace."

"What did you see from the window?" Ted strived to conceal his impatience.

"It was one Friday right after it got dark. A big man drove up in a car. A light blue one. It looked like blue to the wife and me. He took a pick and shovel out of the trunk, and then a big sack. He went with them into the woods, and he didn't come back for almost half an hour. He didn't have the sack when he came out of the woods."

"What does that have to do with Tyrone?" Bill was disappointed.

"It could be the same man," their informer pounced. "That's where the police found the body of that little boy last Sunday morning. In a field beyond those woods. Somebody saw a cap on the ground, and a place nearby where somebody had been diggin'. They weren't planting cotton or corn this time of year."

"Would you recognize him?" Ted asked. "If we brought a lot of pictures, could you pick him out?"

"No. I couldn't do that." He was terrified at the possibility of being put in such a position. "It was dark already. We didn't get a good look at his face."

"Did you get the licence plate number of the car?" Ted probed.

"My goodness, we couldn't see that far away," he clucked. "It musta been a hundred and fifty feet. Our eyes ain't that good no more." He stared eagerly from Ted to Bill. "Do I get the reward money?"

"Give us a real lead and it's yours," Bill said. "We have nowhere to go with this."

"It was a big man in a light blue car," the little man pushed. "Ain't that a help?" But his voice told Laurie his hope was ebbing.

103

"It's not specific enough, it won't lead us anywhere."
Ted was blunt.

"You mean I don't get nothin'?"

"I'll give you a cheque for a hundred dollars," Bill
said. "For your trouble in coming here."

"Can I have it in cash?" he pleaded. "A cheque would
make me awful nervous."

"I'll see what I have on me." Bill reached into
his pocket.

"I have it," Ted said, and pulled out his wallet. "I
cashed a large cheque before I came down here."

Laurie sat immobile. Her mind racing. A big man.
That tied in with her theory that the woman did the
kidnapping, and her husband – or man friend – did the
killings.

Let them dig up the lists from the hospitals and start
checking out mothers who had lost a child in the period
before the kidnappings. This was Wednesday. Tyrone
had been missing since Sunday afternoon. She could not
blot from her mind the fearful reality of the coroner's
report. The last little boy had been killed four to six
days after his disappearance.

They were running out of time.

Chapter Seventeen

Laurie exchanged small talk with the waitress while her poached eggs on toast and coffee was placed before her. Poached because that way she could eat the white and reject the yolks. As the waitress turned to leave, Ted and Bill rose from their booth to join Laurie. Ted indicated to the waitress that she was to bring their orders to Laurie's table.

"Did you hear?" Ted asked.

Laurie nodded.

"Do you believe he wouldn't recognize the man?" She was conscious of the waitress's curiosity that Ted and Bill had joined her.

"He's scared, but he's hungry. If he could pick the guy out of mug shots, he would have," Ted surmised.

"I was hoping he'd give us something to go on." Bill slammed a fist on the table in disappointment. "I feel so damn helpless. Poor little Tyrone out there with God knows what kind of maniac."

"How do we pick out the right 'big man' in the city the size of Aurelia?" Ted gestured defeat. "We can't even check it out through the car he drove. There must be thousands of light blue cars driving about the state."

"Find the woman, and we'll find the man." Again instinct insisted this was the right track. Laurie glanced at the clock. "It's too early to expect to hear from Paul. After a patient is dismissed, the records are shifted from the Pediatrics Floor to the hospital office. He'll have to wait until the office opens. Also, he's checking with Peggy Lane's husband." Bill lifted an eyebrow in enquiry. "Remember Paul talking about the retired police officer who's helping us?"

"So we're waiting again." Bill chafed at delay.

"You said you had appointments at the office," Ted reminded him. He was trying to keep Bill busy so he would have distraction from his fears, Laurie interpreted.

"That's right." Bill ignored the breakfast the waitress slid before him. None of them had an appetite for food this morning.

"When do we meet the psychologist?" Laurie asked.

"At noon. I'll pick you up at the office at about quarter to twelve, Bill," Ted said.

"What's the psychologist's background?" Laurie asked.

Bill launched into a detailed breakdown of Ronald Snyder's substantial career. Clearly Ron was a bright, compassionate man, for whom Bill had enormous respect. They had worked together before Bill and Angie moved to Aurelia, when both were part of a government team in another state and probing into the problems of child abuse.

Despite Bill's restlessness they sat over more cups of coffee and re-explored the situation. Laurie was weighed down by the realization that Bill – and that meant Angie as well – was tying his hopes to the theory that she had brought to them.

"As soon as we have those lists, we'll start moving." Ted squinted in thought. "The more I think of it, Laurie, the more I believe you're right."

"We'll follow through." Laurie was disquieted. Bill and Angie would be devastated if they failed. But they *mustn't* fail. Time was breathing down their necks.

Suppose the woman's child had died in a hospital outside the county? How could they track every hospital for names? All at once the enormity of their undertaking was almost overwhelming.

"Look, there's another angle we ought to try," Ted intruded on her introspection. "We'll finish breakfast. Bill, you go on to the office. Laurie and I will head downtown for the Aurelia Public Library. We'll comb the obituaries. Maybe we'll hit something."

Laurie looked at the clock again. It was barely eight o'clock, despite all their talking.

"The library won't be open at this hour, will it?" Laurie questioned.

"We'll try the newspaper offices instead," Ted decided. "They'll be open."

"I know people on both of the newspapers in town," Bill said. "I might have some short-cuts for you there."

"Call and cut the red tape," Ted ordered. "Laurie will try the files at one newspaper. I'll take the other."

Bill made phone calls. The road was clear for Ted and Laurie to have access to back issues of local newspapers without waiting around. Ted would drive Bill to his office, then head downtown, where the newspapers

107

were located. Laurie would go directly to the offices of the newspaper she was to cover. She'd use Angie's car for the rest of the day.

This was a wild goose chase, Laurie warned herself unhappily while she settled herself behind the wheel of the car. But until they had lists of names to pursue, they were at loose ends. Maybe they would get lucky . . .

Chapter Eighteen

At his first break on the Pediatrics Floor, Paul strode to a telephone to call Frank Lane, Peggy's husband. Frank would take care of the running around, he plotted while the phone rang.

"Good-morning," Frank's deep, cheerful voice came to Paul.

"Hi, Frank. Peggy told me to buzz you," he said swiftly, lest Frank fear a call from him was bad news about Peggy. She was doing fine. She was scheduled to check out of the hospital in three days. "It's Paul Norman here."

"Hi, Doc. Peg called me last night and told me what was going down. I was waiting to hear from you."

"I didn't want to call you at 6.45am," Paul apologized.

"Peggy and I are always up at six. That woman doesn't want to miss anything on this earth." Frank chuckled. "Just tell me what you want me to do, and I'll start hustling."

Keeping his voice low so that passers-by could not overhear, Paul gave him explicit directions.

"Look, you'll be on your own," Paul warned. "I have

contacts only at Aurelia and County General. That's as far as I can go."

"Don't worry about that, Doc," Frank soothed. "We've been living in these parts for years. I was never a police officer right here in Aurelia, but there's a kind of kinship with fellows who've been officers in other parts. And I've been a security guard on and off around here. I know a lot of people, and I know how to get to know them. I'll check with you later in the day. Through Peggy."

"Frank, I do appreciate your efforts."

"Hey, we're all anxious to see this nuttiness stopped. I'm glad to be part of the action."

"We're doing this on our own," Paul reminded. "This isn't a police effort."

"As soon as you have something to show, you'll be taking it to the police," Frank pinpointed. "They're not too proud to accept help. Didn't they bring that psychic down from Chicago? Gee, I never thought I'd see that down in these parts."

"We're running against time," Paul said apprehensively.

"I know that." Frank was sombre. "I'll bring out the bike and get going. Talk to you later."

Paul checked his watch. It was close to nine am. The next break he got he would go downstairs to the chart room and campaign for the list of fatalities on the Pediatrics Floor.

"Dr Norman, please call Emergency. Dr Norman, please call Emergency," a voice came over the speaker system.

*   *   *

110

By the time Paul was in the clear it was well past ten. He swore under his breath. Laurie had probably checked with the motel already to see if he had left a message. He headed for the elevators, irritated at this delay. At last a 'down' elevator stopped on Four, and he darted inside.

Paul strode down the aisle of the administrative wing to the chart room. It would take him forever to check through the Pediatrics charts for the ninety-day period they had pinpointed as crucial, he worried. He couldn't stay off the floor long enough to handle it. If he waited to tackle it on his lunch hour, they'd be losing time. And he never knew when he'd be clear for lunch. That could be three in the afternoon.

Hallie Murphy would pitch in, he plotted with one hand on the door to the chart room. She had been shifted down here two months ago while she battled with an arthritic knee. She was the best pediatrics nurse he'd ever encountered. He sorely missed her on the floor.

"What's the happy young resident doing in this mausoleum?" Hallie greeted him from behind a desk. "You're off your turf."

"So are you," Paul threw back at her. "I can't wait for them to send you back upstairs. What else can I use to frighten those kids into behaving themselves?"

"I should be back in time for Halloween," Hallie drawled. "The wicked witch will be on duty by then."

"Hallie, I need a favour." He used the same ingratiating smile that had subdued Hallie's ire at being faced with back-to-back shifts in recurrent emergencies.

"Why should I do you a favour?" she grumbled, but her eyes were soft.

111

"Because there's nobody else who can do it for me." He dropped onto the corner of her desk. "I'll carry the charts over here for you, and I'll come back down and put them back," he promised. "I need a list of every child who has died on the Pediatrics service between August 1st and October 31st of last year. Names and addresses." He was relieved that it was hospital policy to list addresses on the charts. One less step to worry about.

"That's all?" Hallie lifted her eyebrows. "No cause of death? No attending physician?"

"Name and address," Paul reiterated. "Well, maybe pull out those charts and let me have a fast look at them."

"Might I ask why you want this list? Could it be that young Dr Norman is anxious about a malpractice suit? That kind of excitement we don't need at this hospital."

"No malpractice suit." He was firm. "Just statistics for a report a friend of mine is working on. The hospital won't be mentioned by name," he placated. "Just figures."

"Then why can't I just count and give you the totals?" Hallie countered suspiciously.

"Hallie Murphy, you are a cantankerous old biddy," he scolded. "I need names and addresses for this friend of mine. She has to be able to back up her figures if she's called in to verify them."

"Ah-hah." Hallie's face lighted. "She. A girlfriend working on her master's," she decided. Pleased with this deduction.

"Her Ph.D.," Paul fabricated. Hallie was a romantic

and an educational snob. "Where do I put the charts when I bring them down?" He was already heading for the shelves.

"Pile them up on my desk," Hallie ordered. "But you make sure you get your tail down here later and put them back on the shelves. I'm not into physical labour on this assignment."

"Hallie, you're the love of my life," Paul confided with a grin of satisfaction while he dumped the first batch of charts on Hallie's desk.

"This is only August," she groaned, inspecting the pile. "Was it that heavy a month?"

"It won't take you more than an hour," Paul cajoled. "Quick as you are."

"It'll take me two hours," she judged. "And don't you dare come chasing down here before then."

Paul brought out the September and October charts, deposited a grateful kiss on top of Hallie's head, and dashed from the room. As soon as he had the list, he would phone the motel and leave word for Laurie to call Peggy. Peggy was their liaison officer.

It would be noon before he could check with Hallie, he tabulated. Laurie and Ted would be having lunch with the psychologist. Maybe he'd try Hallie a little before noon, he decided in stubborn optimism. Laurie would check for messages before she went to lunch.

Chapter Nineteen

Laurie sat in a chair beside the desk of the newspaper employee in charge of the microfilm files while the pleasant-faced woman went to pull out the requested rolls of film. Waiting, Laurie allowed her mind to replay the brief encounter in the diner between Bill and Ted and the man who responded to the reward notice.

She was convinced the 'big man in a blue car' was their quarry. How frustrating that the scared little informer could not have nailed down the licence number of the car.

It would be futile to try to check out every blue car registered in Aurelia. The list would be endless. Yet hearing about the man who carried a sack into the woods and emerged without it strengthened Laurie's conviction that she was on the right trail.

Ted and Bill were stopping at police headquarters downtown before going to their individual destinations. They had come to alert the police to the response from the reward notice. They would be truthful when they said they didn't know the name of the informer.

Two people must be involved. A woman, and the man seen going into the woods with a sack that contained the body the police discovered. Had Paul acquired the list of children who had died at Aurelia Hospital in that period? She'd phone the motel as soon as she left the newspaper office.

"Do you need help with the microfilm machine?" the woman enquired with the Southern charm Laurie found so delightful.

"Thank you, no. I'm familiar with them."

She accepted the three rolls of microfilm in their neatly labelled yellow boxes, and headed for the machine put at her disposal. It seemed weeks ago that she had sat in the microfilm room at Columbia's library and read the accounts of the Aurelia kidnappings and murders. *That was only slightly less than forty-eight hours ago.*

She slid the first reel into position, threaded it, and flipped the switch. Moving with compulsive speed through the pages to the obituary section, she knew there was little chance they would find a lead this way. She felt a chill close in about her as her eyes scanned the obituaries, searching for the death of a child.

Methodically, with constant checks on the time, Laurie pushed her way through ninety issues of the newspaper. The only juvenile death reported was that of a little girl who had died in an automobile accident. A little girl who lived with a widowed father. But their hopes on this venture had been meagre, Laurie conceded.

She re-wound the last of the reels, returned it to its box, and took the film to the desk of the woman who had given it to her.

"I hope you found what you wanted." The woman looked up with a cordial smile.

"Thank you, yes," Laurie fabricated. What she wanted was not that easy to come by.

Laurie left the newspaper office, sought a pay telephone. She dialled the motel. Her heart pounded when the switchboard operator told her to call Peggy Lane, and gave her Peggy's phone number at the hospital.

"Lane's Lunatic Rest," Peggy answered blithely and Laurie laughed.

"I feel like Lois Lane without Clark Kent. Right now we need Superman," Laurie said. Her voice wry.

"You've got Paul Norman," Peggy reminded. "In my book he's pretty close to Superman."

"I had a message to check with you."

"Paul wanted you to know he made contact. He'll have the list by noon," Peggy reported. "My old man is out cruising at the other hospitals. He'll come up with more names. You can bet on it."

"I have a luncheon appointment at twelve," Laurie said, "but I'll call from the restaurant."

"That gives you about twenty minutes. Have you got far to travel?"

"I don't think so." Ted had briefed her on distances. "I'm just a block from the *Aurelia Constitution* offices. We're eating at Chez Mario's."

"Ten minutes on foot," Peggy judged. "If you're travelling by car, leave it. You'll go out of your mind looking for a parking space downtown at this hour. Oh, and at Chez Mario's, order the scampi if you're a shrimp freak like me. If you don't like seafood, the chicken marsala is sensational."

"Not fresh shrimp?" Laurie was suddenly hungry.

"Fresh shrimp flown up from Apalachicola. Just like

117

when I was a little girl down in Columbus. You have the scampi. You won't be disappointed. And relax, Sugar – you've got Dr Paul Norman on your side, and that's the nearest thing you'll find to Superman round here. And I don't mind saying I'm praying hard that you find what you're looking for. I'm a tough old bat, except when it comes to kids."

"I'll call just past twelve," Laurie said. "And thanks for playing go-between."

"That's my pleasure and privilege. You and Paul get on your horses and find that little boy!"

Chapter Twenty

Paul tried to offer what meagre encouragement was realistic to the parents of a five-year-old suffering from leukaemia. He had gone into pediatrics because he wanted to work with children, yet each terminal case he encountered became a personal anguish.

Would he ever learn not to become personally involved? There was a point when this was necessary. That he become solely a physician. Yet it was his compassion that had brought him into medicine. It would be forever a part of his make-up. He hoped it would make him a better doctor.

"Thank you, Dr Norman." The little girl's father extended a hand in gratitude. "I know you'll do everything that's humanly possible."

Paul went to the nurses' station to hand over the chart that contained a death sentence. His mind focused now on the Aurelia children who were missing. On Ted Craig's nephew. Just one year older than his small patient with leukemia.

He looked at his watch. It was 11.50am. He had promised Hallie he wouldn't show up before noon. So he'd be a few minutes early. He had officially been on his lunch hour for the last twenty minutes. He would go down to see Hallie before he got paged again.

Paul walked to the elevator, pushed the 'Down' button. Did they have a chance of stopping this massacre? Every weekend dedicated groups of volunteers went out to search. In deserted buildings, empty lots, any place where a small child might be hidden away until a sick mind demanded the child's life.

The police had a task force in operation. Every aid known to science had been brought in. Automated telephone calls to every house, every apartment, within a five-mile radius of the areas where the victims had lived. No leads.

The elevator stopped on Four. Paul walked inside, waited for the elevator to move again. He pushed the lobby button repeatedly. Knowing this had no effect, yet driven to take this small action.

The door slid closed. The elevator made a descent that was interrupted at each floor below, before depositing Paul in the lobby. He pushed his way through the now crowded elevator with an urgency that elicited minor reproach from a visitor.

"Maybe he's on some emergency," the visitor's companion soothed.

This was an emergency, Paul agreed while he hurried down the hall and around the bend to the chart room. Hallie sat at her desk, still going through charts.

"It's not noon yet," she objected. "Don't you know the nurses in this hospital belong to a union?"

"You're almost finished." Paul's eyes swept over the piles of charts. "How are we doing?"

"Depends upon how you see it." Hallie shrugged. "In August we lost five kids. In September eleven. I'm still

120

working on October. You want a lot of names?"

"Hallie, I hope the mortality rate was low," he reproached. "You pulled out those charts?"

"Here . . ." She pointed to a low pile. "The kids who didn't make it."

Paul reached for a piece of paper, pulled a pen from the pocket of his hospital jacket. He picked up the first chart, wrote down the child's name and address. Swiftly he worked through the pulled-out charts, making a note – for possible future use – of the cause of death. Most of the fatalities, he realized, were the result of long-term illnesses.

Laurie said instinct told her that the death they were looking for was unexpected. She was reasoning that a sudden, unexpected death could unhinge a mother. Yet he remembered mothers who had sustained themselves through agonizingly long months of watching a child die, only to fall apart weeks later. Let them check out every name on this list with equal intensity.

"Here's the October crop." Hallie handed over another batch of charts. "What kind of crazy report is your girlfriend working on?" Curiosity was surfacing again.

"Hallie, I told you," Paul chided. "She's doing a doctoral thesis on child mortality figures in this state."

"Why did she pick this hospital?"

"This is just one." Paul was writing down the names and addresses of the October deaths. "She's checking every hospital in the state."

"Why couldn't she do something useful?" Hallie grumbled. "Like a doctoral thesis on whose killing the kids of Aurelia, Alabama?"

Paul looked up with a start. Hallie appeared guile-less.

"Anything new crop up?" he asked. "A news bull-etin?"

"Not that I've heard of," Hallie admitted. "But a couple of our aides live nearby where some of the kids went missing. Both have kids themselves. They're nervous wrecks. And Maria Sanchez on Pediatrics is married to a cop. She says she can't talk to him these days. They're all upset at not being able to catch the creep." She squinted in reflection. "We all keep thinking of the creep as being a man. Wouldn't it be nutty if the killer turned out to be a woman?"

"You got a theory?" Paul began to pile up the charts for return to the shelves. It was four minutes to noon. He'd left word for Laurie that he would have the list by noon. She'd be checking in with Peggy soon.

"It could be a woman," Hallie reiterated. "The way they dress these days you can't tell some of them from men."

"Nobody's seen the kidnapper," Paul reminded her.

"Yes I know, but it could just be a woman who hates kids," Hallie remarked.

Chapter Twenty-One

Laurie left the newspaper office and threaded her way through the midday crowds that thronged the city's downtown business area. It seemed bizarre to her that business continued as usual in a city stalked by a killer.

She thought about the British, and the way they continued their daily lives in the midst of the Blitz. About the cities in Europe that went about the routine of living even while Nazis marched through their streets. Here in Aurelia a child disappeared every twenty-eight days. Nobody knew whose child would be next.

Every parent in Aurelia feared that the next child kidnapped might be theirs. *No* child in Aurelia was safe as long as the kidnapper walked free. And so far there was no real lead, Laurie forced herself to acknowledge. Only the 'big man in a light-blue car'.

Laurie spied a sign about a hundred feet ahead that read, 'Chez Mario's'. A clock in a store window told her it was noon. Subconsciously she quickened her pace. Her eyes searched the cars at the parking meters. Ted and Bill were not here yet. Unless they had parked further down somewhere or at a parking lot.

She could call Peggy now, Laurie decided as she walked into Chez Mario's. Paul said he'd have the list of names by noon. There would be a phone in the restaurant.

A cluster of people were waiting for tables. There seemed to be several rooms. The walls were white-washed, hung with colourful tapestries. Wrought iron chandeliers and wall sconces lent a Mediterranean atmosphere. Candles on each table.

Had Ted or Bill made a reservation? Before she could check this out, she felt a hand on her shoulder. Ted had arrived with Bill and a man in his forties who, Laurie guessed, was Ron Snyder, the psychologist.

"Laurie, this is Ron Snyder," Ted confirmed. "Laurie Roberts."

"Hi, Laurie." Ron Snyder's smile was warm and reassuring. She felt drawn to him instantly. He reminded her of Mark's friend, who had been athletic coach at the school in suburban Boston. Both of them men of medium height, winning the battle against weight. A low-keyed quality about Ron, like the coach, that was comforting.

"I've been eager to meet you." Laurie extended a hand.

"We have a reservation," Ted told her and consulted with a waiter.

They were led to a corner table in a rear room, where some privacy was promised. Laurie was conscious that it was past noon. Paul must have left a message with Peggy by now.

"Bill, would you please order for me?" she asked.

124

Bill knew the cuisine here. "I want to call the hospital. Paul said he would have that list for us by noon."

"You trust him?" Ron teased.

"I trust him," Laurie said. Again she was amazed that they could talk with such lightness when inside they were all so desperate.

"Do you need change?" Ted was fishing in his pocket.

"I have it," Laurie told him.

A waiter directed her to the public telephones. She dialled Peggy's room and waited. Peggy should be there, she thought in sudden worry. Lunch trays came to the rooms at noon.

"Hello, Lane's Lunatic Rest," Peggy's voice came to her after a dozen rings.

"It's Laurie—" She was breathless with anticipation. A list of names would propel them into action.

"Paul just walked out," Peggy told her. "He said to tell you he's leaving an envelope for you at the downstairs' desk. He left it down there to save you time. If anything goes haywire and they misplace it, I have a copy up here."

"We're at the restaurant right now with Dr Snyder. He's the psychologist," Laurie said in sudden ambivalence. Ought she to rush over to the hospital right now and pick up that list?

"Have your lunch and talk to the psychologist." Peggy read her mind. "You'll get the list as soon as you've picked his brain. And I hope you're having something better than what they're serving us for lunch. I'm in the mood for spaghetti and garlic bread, and what do we have? Broiled cod, mashed potatoes, and string

125

beans. With tapioca for dessert. I had something like spumoni in mind."

"We'll have spaghetti and garlic bread and spumoni when you're sprung," Laurie promised affectionately. "And an antipasto and a gorgeous salad."

"For that I might spring myself." Peggy giggled. "Oh, remember Frank's out rustling up other lists. You'll have plenty to keep you busy tomorrow."

"Peggy, you're wonderful. I'd better run now."

For a moment Laurie stood before the phone. Paul had one list. Frank was picking up others. But this was Wednesday, and Tyrone had been missing since Sunday afternoon. Almost seventy hours. *Could they find that woman in time*?

Laurie returned to their table. The three men were in earnest conversation. Their voices low to keep the privacy.

"Paul has the list," she said as she sat down. "I'll pick it up right after lunch. Peggy's husband is out checking with the other hospitals. We'll have lots of names by tonight." It was frightening to realize how much ground they must cover. "Paul suggested we each check in with Peggy at two hour intervals."

"Right," Ted agreed, and Bill nodded. "We'll go with you to pick up the first list and divide the names between us. We can start right out."

"It worries me that we don't find these people before their minds break down," Ron said. "Oh, we see a lot of them," he acknowledged. "But it's the ones we don't see who erupt into disaster. The professionals – those in psychology and psychiatry – should have

126

a medium to instruct laymen to recognize the danger signals."

"You mean we should see the developing signs of mental disturbances in friends and relatives?" Laurie asked. "And that way get them into treatment?"

"Right." Ron nodded. His face reflected both sympathy and frustration. "It would be a great deterrent to violent crimes. I'm not saying people should be shunted into therapy at any sign of temporary emotional upset, but we should have legal ways to bring the genuinely troubled person into a helping situation. For his own sake and that of possible victims."

"Perhaps the woman who took Tyrone – if what Laurie suspects is true – was in therapy?" Bill clutched at a fresh avenue. "How can we follow up that angle?"

"The relationship between psychologist or psychiatrist and patient is inviolate. You can't go asking for case histories." Ron hesitated. "But I suspect that any psychologist or psychiatrist in Aurelia – knowing what's happening here – would feel a moral obligation to consult with the police if he or she suspected a patient capable of being guilty of taking these children."

"What questions should we put to these women we're approaching?" Doubts tugged at Laurie now. On a routine interview she knew what questions to ask. But these were not interviews for a magazine article. Lives depended on what information they could elicit. "How can we recognize a possible suspect?"

"First of all," Ron pinpointed, "what are you using to gain admittance?"

"We'll say we're doing a survey on families who've suffered the loss of a child." Laurie had worked this much out. "I know it sounds callous, but we'll explain we're preparing a report to help families survive the terrible period following such a loss." She tensed at the anguish she saw in Bill's eyes as he absorbed what she was saying. But Tyrone was all right. So far. The children were kept alive for a few days. That was the pattern.

"Play it low-keyed," Ron advised. "You may encounter some violent reactions."

"What should we watch for?" Ted asked. "What are the signs that'll identify the woman we're looking for?"

"She'll over-react to questions about children," Ron said. "She'll probably fantasize. But she *believes* these fantasies. She'll talk with total sincerity. She may even talk about a dead child as still being alive. She'll even count miscarriages as live children."

"What else?" Laurie probed, but they were temporarily derailed by the waiter's arrival with a tray of food.

Over a superb luncheon Ron Snyder clued the others in to the signs for which they must be on the look out, signposts they must not ignore. Everyone at the table conscious that time was their enemy. The atmosphere heavy with the portent of this meeting.

"What would you like for dessert?" Bill asked Laurie when the waiter returned with pad and pen.

"Could we settle for coffee?" Laurie asked. "I think

128

we ought to pick up that list of names at the hospital and start following up on these women."

"Coffee for four," Ron ordered briskly. "If there's anything else I can do," he added when the waiter withdrew, "call me. Any time of day or night."

Chapter Twenty-Two

Laurie drove to the hospital, with Ted and Bill trailing her in Bill's car. At the information desk in the lobby she asked for the envelope Paul had left for her. Ted and Bill were coming through the lobby's revolving door as she ripped open the envelope.

Her eyes scanned the list of names and addresses. She knew they were arriving at the critical point in their search. Dividing the list between the three of them they ought to be able to cover the area today, Laurie told herself. Providing all of the women were at their apartments.

"Is this going to be a heavy deal?" Ted was slightly breathless as he arrived at her side. His eyes sought the list she held in one hand.

"This is the first list," she reminded. "Frank Lane will bring in the others later today." If Tyrone wasn't found by five this afternoon, he would be missing three days. *In the next twenty-four hours they had to track him down.* That was the danger point – tomorrow afternoon at five. If the killer stuck to his pattern. She would not allow herself to think that he might accelerate that schedule.

131

"Let's move." Bill was brusque in his anxiety. "We'll break down the list out in the car."

Laurie slid behind the wheel of Angie's car while Ted and Bill divided up the list so that the names Laurie was to approach would be clustered in a small area. She would avoid any difficulty in locating apartments.

The two men left to return to Bill's car. With her list on the seat beside her, Laurie waited for Bill to lead the way through downtown Aurelia to the apartment block she was to approach. She remembered she was to have dinner again tonight with Paul. If she ran late, she would phone and explain.

Laurie was tense behind the wheel. Fearful of losing Bill in the heavy traffic. She was relieved when they moved out onto a less dense highway. Now she focused mentally on her approach to the first woman on her list. Ron had warned that reaching the woman they sought could be dangerous. But she would not allow herself to think about that.

Soon the cluster of red brick buildings that formed the housing estate came into view. Ted waved a hand out the window to indicate this was where she was to turn off. Bill and he were driving on to the next group of buildings where they would begin their search.

Laurie swung off the highway onto the road that led to the wide parking area. She parked, pulled out the ignition key, locked the doors. Her heart was pounding when she walked, with briefcase under arm, to the entrance of the first building. She squinted near-sightedly at the number above the door. Not this building.

A pair of small girls on skateboards paused to inspect her with curiosity.

"Where will I find Number Three?" she asked. Seeing them with fresh awareness.

One of these two little girls might be the next victim. Unless somebody got lucky and nailed the kidnapper and killer. A coldness closed in about her.

"Three's over there." One of the girls pointed. "Are you from Welfare?"

"No." Laurie smiled.

"Probation officer?" the other asked.

"No," Laurie said gently. "I'm a magazine writer." That much was true. Somewhere along the line she must come up with a substantial story for Jim Turner.

Laurie smiled again and walked towards the building designated as Number Three.

She walked into the small entrance foyer of the tall brick building. At her left were the buzzers, with names and apartment numbers indicated.

Though she knew the name at the top of her list, she double-checked. Here it was. Jefferson. Only one family named Jefferson was listed. Apartment 4-C. She pushed the button, gearing herself for the interview ahead.

When there was no response, she rang again. Still no one answered. It was naïve to expect these women to be home because it was so urgent for her to talk with them. They could be downstairs in the laundry room, out shopping at a supermarket, involved in any one of a myriad of tasks that occupy a housewife.

When no answering buzz responded to her second

effort, Laurie hesitated. She was here. Before approaching the next woman on her list, let her make an effort to track down this mother.

A pair of teenagers were opening the door to the vestibule. One had a key in her hand.

"I'm trying to get in to see Mrs Jefferson," Laurie said, "but she doesn't answer. I think her buzzer may not be working."

"Mrs Jefferson's been away for two weeks. Staying with her mother," one of the girls explained. "Her husband won't be home until tonight. He works over at the bakery down the road."

"What do you want to talk to her for?" the girl with the key was not unlocking the door. *She* was a stranger, Laurie realized, and therefore suspect.

"I'm doing a magazine story about child mortality and how families learn to cope with such a painful loss," Laurie improvised. "I understand Mrs Jefferson lost a little girl a few months ago."

"It was awful. She died of cancer after they cut off her leg. All her hair fell out from what they did to her at the hospital. Mrs Jefferson – even if she was home – wouldn't want to talk about it."

"You're sure she's not here?" Laurie tried again.

"Now ain't that the pits!" the other girl exploded. "It's like with the TV news people. Always buttin' in to talk to some poor slob who's been through somethin' awful like losin' somebody in a fire or a car accident or somethin'. You'd better clear out of here, lady. We got enough troubles around here without spillin' our guts to nosey magazine and newspaper people."

"I'm sorry," Laurie stammered. They were right,

134

of course. But how else would they be able to track down the woman who took Tyrone? "It's just that the whole country is shocked about what's happening here in Aurelia. People want to help."

"My cousin was the fourth kid that got snatched. They found her floatin' in a pond. She'd been hit over the head and thrown into the water to drown. Don't bother us, lady. We got enough troubles without you."

The two girls were waiting for her leave before they unlocked the door. They were not going to allow her to go up to the Jeffersons' apartment. Maybe they were telling her the truth. Maybe Mrs Jefferson was out of town. Later she'd try to reach her by phone.

"I hope they find the killer soon," Laurie said. "Everybody's praying for that."

Laurie left Building Three and headed for the one next door. She consulted the doorbells, rang at the second name on her list. Anderson. Apartment 7-H. She lunged for the doorknob as someone in the apartment buzzed to give her admittance. There was no intercom system here whereby a tenant who pushed a buzzer could enquire about the identity of the caller.

The apartment was on the seventh floor. She walked to the elevator and went inside. Feeling uneasy that she was alone. She pushed the button for the seventh floor, and the elevator began its ascent.

She left the elevator and walked down the hall towards a door that was just cracked. A woman peered out behind the meagre protection of a chain.

"Mrs Anderson?" Laurie enquired.

"Yeah." The woman was wary. "If you're selling something, we're not buying."

"I'm not selling anything," Laurie said softly. "I'm researching for a magazine article." She steeled herself to explain the subject. Dreading the fresh pain this would elicit from Mrs Anderson. "It's about how families learn to cope with grief. The most painful grief of all. Losing a child."

"That's something I know about, Miss . . ." She was releasing the chain.

"Laurie Roberts," she introduced herself. "I won't take much of your time."

"Come on in and I'll fix us some coffee." The small, rotund woman, appearing about forty, pulled the door wide.

Laurie walked into the tiny, box-like living room that was neat and comfortable. The unattractive tiles of the floor were masked in part by a red shag rug. The furniture was mail order type maple with cheerful slipcovers. The walls displayed groupings of framed snapshots taken on special occasions. A wedding, christening, a high school graduation photograph, a picnic.

Mrs Anderson seemed to be coping with her grief. But she mustn't jump to conclusions, Laurie exhorted herself. Listen to what Mrs Anderson had to say. Watch for telltale signs.

"That's Thelma's picture there." Mrs Anderson pointed to a photograph on an end table beside the sofa. "That was taken just a few months before we lost her." Her eyes grew bright with grief. "She was my baby. Just seven. I thank the Lord for my four other kids. My two grandchildren. They helped me from going crazy when I lost my baby." She turned away to hide the tears that welled in her eyes. "You sit down, Miss Roberts. I'll bring us coffee. I always got a pot warming on the stove."

Laurie fought against guilt while she waited in the scrupulously clean living room for Mrs Anderson to return. Instinct told her this was not their quarry, yet she knew she must follow through.

Ron said the woman they sought might have fantasies. She might talk about children that didn't exist. Mrs Anderson claimed to have four other children, two grandchildren. Was this a fantasy? No, Laurie rejected, looking at the family photographs about the walls.

Over strong coffee Mrs Anderson talked about her children. Thelma had died of pneumonia. Now every cold became a major alarm. The phone rang and Mrs Anderson excused herself to answer it.

Laurie sat back while Mrs Anderson talked to a friend.

"Oh, Charlie's over his sore throat," Mrs Anderson said. "He's back in school now. And Hilda's sticking with the night school. She means to get that high school equivalency diploma . . ."

Mrs Anderson was not fantasizing. She was a normal, caring woman, struggling to continue her life despite the grief that would never completely release her. This was not the woman they sought.

Chapter Twenty-Three

Lottie ran the iron over the small white shirt draped across the ironing board. She gave the neckline, with the name tag sewed neatly in place – Tyrone Randolph – an extra, loving press. Tyrone was such a nice name.

This morning, while Gus slept, she had gone over to the shopping centre and bought a new shirt for Tyrone and a bright red jacket. He'd look real cute in that jacket. It would be warmer than the baseball jacket he lost when she picked him up and took him off. As cold as it was, he shoulda been wearin' that jacket, instead of lettin' it lay there on the pavement.

Lottie's face softened as she visualized him pulling off the jacket in a fit of rage. The other – bigger – kids had raced off on skateboards and left him alone. That was the minute she had been waiting for. A handkerchief with ethyl chloride over his nose for a minute and he went right out.

Now the skillet on the stove captured her attention. The kitchen was warm this morning because she had turned on all the burners of the kerosene stove, though she was using only one. She liked the kerosene smell in the kitchen; it reminded her of when she was a little girl, living here with Mama and Papa and her sisters and brothers and grandmother.

Mama was always cookin', Lottie reminisced. Somebody was always comin' into the kitchen to eat. From a job in town, or school, or from out in the fields. A long time ago they raised cotton in the fields. Now Mama and Papa and Grandma were buried out back, and her brothers and sisters had moved away to Montgomery and Mobile.

Gus kept sayin' he'd buy her a stove from Sears that would use bottled gas, but she didn't mind. It was Gus who hated the smell of kerosene. She reached for a spatula to flip the hamburger in the skillet over to the uncooked side, crossed to the table to slice the bun that sat there in readiness.

The chocolate puddin' would be nice and cool now, she decided. Tyrone would like that. All kids like chocolate puddin'. She brought the dish of chocolate pudding from the refrigerator and turned to the clock. She knew exactly when the medicine would wear off to the point where Tyrone would wake up enough to eat.

He would be groggy but hungry. He'd be her little boy, and she'd feed him. Before he woke up too much, she'd give him that tiny little prick in the arm that would put him back to sleep again.

She brought out the tray Gus had bought for her at the county fair last year, lined it with a pink napkin. She was singing under her breath when she lifted up the hamburger to see if it was brown enough on the other side.

With the laden tray in her hands she climbed up to

the second floor. She put down the tray to open the door to the bedroom she shared with Gus. he was still asleep. The fire in the grate was almost out. She'd have to throw on some more coal when she had fed the baby.

Lottie debated a moment, then slid the hook into the eye on the bedroom door. Gus wouldn't wake up, but it made her feel better to know he was locked in there.

She climbed the stairs to the attic, breathless with the effort. Clutching the tray precariously in one hand. Tyrone was restless. That meant he'd be opening his eyes any minute now. She put the tray on the floor beside the cot and waited for him to wake.

"Mommie . . ." He whimpered as he returned to reality. "Mommie . . ."

"Ssh," Lottie soothed. "Everythin's just fine. I brought a hamburger. Lots of ketchup on it. You sit up and eat it now."

"I want my Mommie . . ." Tyrone was not fully awake.

Lottie lowered herself to the cot and pulled him into her lap.

"Take a bit of the hamburger," she urged. "It's real good." He was still half-asleep, but the aroma of the hamburger captured his interest.

Under Lottie's coaxing he ate half of the hamburger, then allowed her to spoon the chocolate pudding into his mouth.

"Mommie . . ." He was emerging from the lethargy of the medication. "I want my Mommie!" He was struggling now in her arms.

"Sssh." Terror filled her. She wouldn't let Gus

find out about this one. She was keeping Tyrone. He was her little boy. "Sssh." With one practised hand she reached on the upturned orange crate for the hypodermic needle. A fast prick of his arm and he was already relaxing. In a minute he'd be asleep again.

She put him down on the bed, covered him with the quilt, and adjusted the kerosene stove that kept the temperature in the room at a comfortable range. She was singing softly as she moved down the stairs:

> "Sweetes' lil' feller—
> Everybody knows . . ."

She paused at the door of the bedroom and lifted the hook from the eye. With cautious slowness lest Gus hear and become suspicious. But he didn't know about Tyrone sleepin' upstairs, she told herself.

When was Gus goin' on that long haul to California? Tomorrow? He didn't say a word about when he'd be leavin'. If he found out about Tyrone, he'd take her baby away. She'd lose him, too. *She didn't want to lose Tyrone.*

She started down to the kitchen. Gus would be hungry when he woke up. She was soaking the slices of salt pork in molasses and water. He always liked fried salt pork with creamy gravy and black-eyed peas. And she had a molasses pecan pie all ready to throw into the oven. They still had pecans from the pickin' last November. The ground had been just loaded with 'em this time.

"Lottie!" Gus's voice echoed from the bedroom. For a moment she flinched, fearful that he'd wake Tyrone. No need to worry, she consoled herself – nothin' was gonna wake Tyrone till the medicine wore off again. "Lottie!"

"I'm comin', Gus," she called. She put down the tray and climbed the stairs again.

Gus was sitting up in bed when she opened the door. He had pulled one of the quilts around him.

"Throw some coal in the grate, Lottie. I'm freezin' to death in here."

"All right, Gus." She went over to the coal scuttle, picked it up and dumped small chunks of coal onto the grate. Maybe a few pieces of kindling would hurry it up, she decided, and reached for a few sticks of the greasy kindling wood. "You hungry, Gus?"

"Not yet. I've been thinkin'. Maybe I'll buy a Franklin stove and set it up in here. That'll keep you warm when I'm away," he kidded in sudden good humour.

"When are you leavin' on that California trip?" she asked while she worked at restoring the fire in the grate.

"Soon enough," he said.

"How soon?" she pushed. It made her nervous, having Gus in the house now. He didn't trust her. But he didn't know about Tyrone up in the attic. She'd always kept them in the other bedroom until she thought about buyin' a kerosene stove for up in the attic. Why hadn't she thought about that before? "Gus . . ."

"You gonna miss the old man?" She saw the amorous glow in his eyes.

"What difference does it make?" Involuntarily she was defiant. "It don't mean nothin' when you're home. It's like we was strangers."

"Honey, you come here into the bed and tell me we're strangers," he challenged.

"You won't do anythin'," she accused.

"Come on over here," he ordered. "Get under the covers with your old man."

She looked at the grate for an instant to make sure the fire would catch again, then went over to the bed. She felt the springs creak beneath her weight.

"Lottie, don't I take good care of you?" he demanded. "All them pretty dolls I keep bringin' you?" His body moved against hers. He was gettin' all worked up, she thought. But it wasn't natural, the way he'd just hold her and rub up against her. He used to brag about how good she was when they made love. "But you're the prettiest doll in the world . . ."

She heard the grunt of passion low in his throat. Tonight was going to be different, she told herself in soaring anticipation. He was talkin' crazy – the way he always did when they used to make love.

For a little while Lottie was happier than she had been in many months. The fire in the grate was throwing warmth into the room with a strength that reached the bed. And Gus was bringing himself to her. Her arms clung to him while they rocked together. *Oh Gus, you're givin' me a baby! You're givin' me a baby!*

But all at once Gus was pulling away. She turned cold with shock.

"Gus," she sobbed. "You promised me. You promised me!"

Chapter Twenty-Four

The third name on Laurie's list was Carleton. She went to the building given as the Carletons' address. In the carbon copy vestibule she scanned the names beside the doorbells. There was no Carleton on the name plates.

Laurie left the building and sought out the apartment office. A helpful clerk checked out the Carletons' apartment once Laurie insisted they were residents.

"You were in the wrong building," the pleasant young woman explained. "She's in Building One. Apartment 6-M."

"That's the only Carleton in the building?" Laurie probed. Chafing at wasted time.

"Just one," the young woman confirmed. "Apartment 6-M." Now she proceeded to give Laurie directions.

"Thank you." Laurie smiled in gratitude and left the office.

Concentrating on the directions the clerk in the office had given her, Laurie sought for Building One. Within a few minutes she was standing, tired from tension, in the vestibule of Building One. Her eyes ran down the names beside the bells. Here it was. Carleton. 6-M.

She rang the bell and waited. She was about to concede that Mrs Carleton wasn't home when the buzzer rang with a jarring intensity. Continuing to ring even after she was inside the door and at the elevator.

At the sixth floor she left the elevator and walked down the cold, unattractive corridor, inspecting apartment numbers. Here it was. A Christmas wreath still hung on the door. Was that an indication of something?

She looked for a name plate on the door. No name. Only the number of the apartment. She rang and waited. She heard the sound of the television set inside. Mrs Carleton was watching a soap opera.

"Who is it?" a voice asked from behind the closed door.

"My name is Laurie Roberts. I'd like to interview you for a research project. It'll take only a few minutes. I have identification," Laurie added. "I've just spoken with Mrs Anderson in Building Two."

"Oh, her." Contempt laced the woman's voice. "You'd think she was the only woman who ever lost a kid."

The door opened. A tall, model-thin young woman with stringy blonde hair stood there. She wore what appeared to be a maternity dress, though she wasn't showing. Her fingernails were abnormally long, painted a violent red.

"I'd like to talk to you about how women handle their grief in such a situation. It's for a magazine article."

"What magazine?" Mrs Carleton seemed intrigued.

"*Manhattan Weekly*," Laurie told her.

"Why are you interviewing women down here?" Now Mrs Carleton sounded hostile.

"We're doing research in four different sections of the country," Laurie fabricated. "Aurelia is the Southern city the publisher chose. May I come in and talk to you for a few minutes?"

"OK." She shrugged. "The other kids are all asleep. Why not?" She pulled the door wide. "I'm Dinah."

"Thank you for seeing me, Dinah." Laurie walked into the sparsely furnished living room. Warning signals jogged up in her mind. Dinah Carleton said the other children were all asleep. This was clearly a one-bedroom apartment. The door to the bedroom was closed. Locked, Laurie noticed. A special lock had been installed. What was Dinah Carleton hiding in that room? *Who* was she hiding?

"I'll turn off the TV." Dinah crossed to switch off the soap opera. "Sit down."

The only furniture in the living room was a mattress covered by a paisley throw, a fringed floor lamp that sat at one end of the mattress, and the television set. Several empty beer bottles lay in a corner of the room.

"I know it's painful to talk about losing a child," Laurie began, sitting at the edge of the bed.

"Hey, you don't know what pain is until you've lost a kid. That's why I'm so watchful over the others. They're sleeping now. There in the bedroom." She pointed to the locked door. "Two boys and two girls. I keep the door locked so nobody can go in there and hurt them. You know about what's been happening to

149

children here in this area?"

"Yes." Laurie nodded. Was Tyrone in that room? Were other missing children in there with him?

"It's good that you have other children." Laurie was uneasy. Something about Dinah Carleton's face, her eyes, told her this woman was unbalanced.

"I'm having another one soon." Dinah stared at her in defiance. "You don't believe me, do you? They all laugh at me. They don't believe I'm going to have another baby."

"Of course I believe it," Laurie soothed. She ought to get out of this apartment. *Fast*.

"No, you don't." Dinah glowed in rage. "You're just like all the others. You don't believe I'm pregnant. Just because I lost Millie, you think I can't have another baby. But I'm going to have another one. Next month!" Rage changed to triumph.

"How lovely for you." Was Tyrone and the other missing children in the bedroom? But not a sound emerged. They might be drugged. "I think it's just wonderful."

"No, you don't! You're laughing at me. Just like all the others. Just because Jasper walked out on me when I lost Millie. But he left me a present. He left me another baby. You want me to lose it, don't you? *Jasper sent you here*. He wants you to beat me up so I'll lose the baby!"

"No, Dinah." Laurie rose to her feet. Gauging the distance to the door.

"Don't lie to me!" Dinah threw herself at Laurie. The long red nails ripped at Laurie's face. "I know why you're here! Don't lie to me!"

Laurie fought to free herself from Dinah's flailing hands. She stumbled and fell across the bed. Dinah was instantly hovering above her, intent on physical damage. Now Laurie took the offensive. Averting her face to avoid more scratches, she captured Dinah's wrists, swung her onto her back.

"You want me to lose the baby!" Dinah wailed. "Don't beat me up! I don't want to miscarry!"

"Nobody's going to beat you up, Dinah." Cautiously Laurie loosened her hold on Dinah's wrists. Dinah began to sob inconsolably. "You just lie there and rest," Laurie soothed. "You're going to be fine."

Laurie released Dinah's wrists and arose from the bed. She moved towards the door, wary of a fresh attack. But Dinah seemed no longer aware of her presence.

Laurie pulled the door wide, closed it behind her, and hurried down the hall. She took the stairs rather than risk waiting for the elevator. She was conscious that her face was bleeding. She was trembling from the encounter.

Though Dinah Carleton was a disturbed mother who had lost a child, Laurie did not believe she was guilty of kidnapping the Aurelia children. But Dinah had given her a fresh insight. They had been searching for a mother whose child had died. Now instinct told her that the woman they sought might have lost a child through miscarriage.

They must search for a woman who had miscarried shortly before the first child was kidnapped. A woman who suffered fresh torment each time she began to menstruate again. *To that woman the arrival of another menstrual period was equivalent to another miscarriage.*

Laurie rushed from the building and towards the parking area. She must get to the hospital and talk to Paul. Time was so short for Tyrone.

Chapter Twenty-Five

In the car Laurie paused to dab a tissue at the jagged scratches on her face. Impatient at her ineffectual efforts to erase the signs of the attack on her, she abandoned this to reach for the ignition key. No time to waste on such niceties.

At the hospital she went up to the Pediatrics Floor. No one questioned her; this was visiting hours. But she felt the curious stares of the three women in the elevator with her as she self-consciously held a tissue against the side of her face that bore the brunt of Dinah's attack.

The nurse on duty at the nurses' station recognized her. She had been here when Laurie arrived early this morning after the call from Paul.

"You're hurt," the nurse said, her eyes fastened to the bleeding scratches on Laurie's face.

"It's nothing," Laurie dismissed this. "Do you suppose I could see Dr Norman for a moment? It's terribly important."

"I'll page him," she said, and reached for the mike. "But those scratches should be cleaned up. You could develop a bad infection."

Laurie waited while Paul was paged. Still shaky

from the battle with Dinah Carleton. Now she asked herself if she was jumping to conclusions about another approach to the kidnapper. *Was Tyrone there in Dinah Carleton's apartment*? Maybe they ought to call off everything else and put all their efforts into checking out Dinah Carleton. Time was so short.

Laurie spied Paul charging down the hall at his customary speed.

"Laurie!" His face showed his alarm. "What happened?"

"It's nothing," she said. "Let's go some place where we can talk."

"Laurie, I don't like this," he protested, his eyes inspecting the ugly scratches. "I know it's early to be talking this way, but you're important in my life." He took her by the arm and prodded her around the bend in the hall.

"I had a run-in with Dinah Carleton," Laurie said when they were beyond the hearing of those at the nurses' station. She tried to sound casual. "One of the names on my list. Dinah's fantasizing about having four other kids. Besides the one who died here in the hospital. I'm convinced she's unbalanced."

"Let me clean up your face." Paul guided her into a small examining room, pushed her into a chair, and proceeded to disinfect the scratches.

"Paul—" Laurie began but he hushed her up.

"Be quiet while I finish up here." He was silent for a few moments, absorbed in his work. "Laurie, I'll have two weeks off in April. I have to spend a few days at home and another day talking with Dr Collier about joining him in practice. If I come to New York for the rest of my time off, will you save some evenings and the weekend for me?" His eyes seemed to be trying to memorize her features.

"I'll save them all," she promised. Knowing Paul belonged in her life.

She sat still while he paused to inspect the results of his ministrations. But her mind returned to Dinah Carleton. She was wrong about concentrating on Dinah. Instinct guided her again.

"Paul, I don't think Dinah's the woman we're looking for."

"Why not?" He tensed in anticipation.

"She said something that made me think we've overlooked one angle. She's convinced she's pregnant and sure that Jasper – I suppose that's her husband – wants her to miscarry . . ."

"You believe the woman we're looking for suffered a miscarriage? And she steals a child to replace the one she had been carrying?"

"I know it's rough to change course now. But couldn't we look for her through hospital charts?"

"We can track down women who've suffered miscarriages." He was thoughtful. "Even if they haven't come here to the hospital, a termination of pregnancy would show up in the prenatal clinic records."

"How fast can we do this?"

"I expect Frank in any minute with the lists we asked for through other hospitals. I'll make some calls and shift him to lists of terminated pregnancies in that period. It'll take time . . ."

He was apprehensive.

"Peggy hasn't heard from Ted or Bill?"

"I talked to her twenty minutes ago. She'd heard nothing." He hesitated. "We should let them follow through on what they're doing. This could go either way."

"I know." But Laurie was convinced that a chart that mentioned a terminated pregnancy would give them the name they needed.

"Let me call downstairs for the Carleton chart. I took names before – I didn't take time out to see the cause of deaths." Paul reached for the phone. "Once I've seen that, we'll go downstairs and check the obstetrical records."

Within minutes an aide walked in and gave him the Carleton child's chart.

"All right, let's see what we have here." For a few moments he concentrated on the chart.

Laurie watched his face for some indication of what he was thinking. Dinah fit the profile Ron had told them to watch for, yet she could not believe that Tyrone was concealed in that apartment. Emotionally she could not believe it. Intellectually she realized that Tyrone – and other missing children – might have been lying in that other room, silenced by drugs.

"It's not Dinah Carleton," Paul said with authority, putting aside the chart. "She had a two-year-old girl who died of a severe beating." His face tightened. "I remember. I talked with the detectives that were brought to the hospital. The man the Carleton woman was living with beat the little girl so badly she didn't have a chance of survival. The mother became deranged. She's an out-patient in the psychiatric department now. She never leaves the house except to come for treatment."

Laurie shuddered. "What kind of a monster beats a child?"

"It's reaching almost epidemic proportions throughout the country," Paul told her. "Families live under such stress these days. If we could reach the parents before they snap, we could save some of these children." Paul rose to his feet. "Let's go down to the chart room and look for a terminated pregnancy."

They hurried in silence to the elevator. Both tense in the knowledge that a breakthrough might be imminent. And all the while Laurie fought against panic. *Time was running out.*

It seemed an interminably long wait, though it was less than three minutes, before they were racing down the lobby floor corridors to the chart room. The nurse at the desk looked up at Paul with exaggerated patience. Laurie was aware that she herself was being given a covert appraisal.

"This is for you, Hallie." Paul handed over the Carleton chart. He grinned at Hallie's hardly subtle interest in Laurie. "This is Laurie Roberts, from New York. Laurie, this is Hallie Murphy, the best damned pediatrics nurse I've ever encountered."

"The Ph.D. candidate?" Hallie lifted her eyebrows in enquiry.

"Hallie, I lied a little," he confessed. "We're trying to track down a killer."

"From the pediatrics charts?" she snorted. "You've been reading too many novels about weird kids."

"We can't waste time – I'll tell you the whole story later. Laurie and I will take you out for the best steak dinner in Aurelia," he promised. "As soon as we nail this thing down."

"What do you want?" Hallie responded to their sense of urgency.

"We want to go through the clinic prenatal charts for August, September, and October of last year," he said.

"Paul, Laurie isn't hospital personnel." Hallie was uncomfortable.

"For today she is," Paul insisted. "Let's say I hired her. I want to go back there and pull out the charts. We have to find a woman who's pregnancy was terminated during those months. We'll split the charts into three piles. You'll help?"

"Do I have any choice?" Hallie grumbled. "These doctors who think they're Sherlock Holmes."

Paul brought out the prenatal charts, divided them into three piles. He showed Laurie what she was to look for without wasting time. She immediately went to work.

The three of them studied the charts with painful intensity. Writing down the names and addresses of prenatal clinic patients who had aborted.

"Paul, this is strange . . ." Laurie felt an inchoate excitement, though reason cautioned there might be a rational explanation for the situation.

"What's strange?" Paul asked. Hallie, too, was attentive.

"This woman attended the prenatal clinic regularly for four months. Then she never showed up again."

"No mention of a terminated pregnancy?" Paul asked.

"The last entry just reports on her visit at the fourth month. Nothing else."

"She could have moved away," Hallie rationalized.

"Let me see the chart." Paul took it from her. "Lottie Johnson. Age twenty-eight. Second pregnancy. On a four-week schedule. She came regularly through the fifth month of pregnancy. Never showed up again."

"She might have aborted at home and never bothered coming in to the hospital," Hallie contributed.

"Let's check her out," Laurie pleaded. Warning signals were popping up in her brain again. *They were close.* "Don't ask me why – I just have a hunch she's the woman. She has Tyrone."

Paul debated an instant and reached for the phone. He was scheduled to go off duty, but he wanted to be sure the resident due to follow him was on the floor.

"OK, I'm clear. Hallie, we've gone through most of the charts. Will you finish up and hold the list for us?"

"I get out of here in twenty minutes," Hallie reminded.

"You'll have time. Send the list up to Pediatrics. I'll pick it up when we come back to the hospital. Hallie, I love you." He leaned forward to kiss her on one cheek.

"You say that to all the nurses," Hallie complained. "Let me know what you find out," she called after him as he took Laurie by the hand and rushed towards the door.

Chapter Twenty-Six

A low hanging fog was settling over the grounds as Laurie and Paul emerged from the hospital. The temperature had been rising for the last two hours, lending an unseasonable spring-like atmosphere to the early dusk.

"Let's take Angie's car," Laurie suggested.

"I'll drive," Paul said. "I know the roads here better than you do."

"Right." Laurie handed him the car keys and pointed to Angie's Pontiac.

Paul unlocked the door for Laurie, then hurried around to the other side. Laurie consulted her watch.

"It's a short drive from here to the apartment, isn't it?"

"Twelve minutes at the most. We've got the building number where Lottie Johnson lives. The chart didn't give the apartment number, but we'll find it on the doorbells."

The highway was beginning to be clogged with homebound workers. The fog slowed the traffic to a crawl. Paul swore at the stop-and-go pace necessitated by the bad visibility.

"Laurie, look in the glove compartment and see if

there's a cloth to clean off the windshield." The wipers were not working.

Laurie opened the compartment, discovered a square of soft material and handed it to Paul. He took advantage of a traffic jam just ahead to get out of the car and clear up the windshield. Laurie saw a small camera tucked inside the compartment. She reached to inspect it.

Angie and Bill were serious about photography, she noted with respect. Did the roll of film inside the camera hold photographs of Tyrone? Her throat tightened. Let them be able to finish that roll with more photographs of their son.

Cars down the line began to move again. Paul hurried back behind the wheel. Laurie knew that he, too, was anxious about Tyrone's well-being. Tyrone had been missing for seventy-two hours. Tomorrow would be the fourth day.

At last Paul swung off onto the short road that led to the apartment block. They parked. Laurie and Paul ran to the building given as Lottie Johnson's address.

"This is it." Laurie's breath quickened in anticipation.

Paul pulled open the door that led into the vestibule. They scanned the names beside the doorbells.

"No Johnsons here," Paul said. He frowned. "We double-checked the address."

"Could she have moved?"

"Let's go to the apartment office and ask." Paul reached for Laurie's hand.

They walked with compulsive haste. Night was fast

approaching. The walks were crowded with home-coming tenants. Lights glowed in every apartment, providing a specious air of safety.

But no children played outdoors despite the spring-like weather. No child dared. Except one teenager careering before them on a skateboard.

"Roger!" A woman's voice yelled from a third floor window. "You come right inside this minute!"

"It looks as though the office is closed," Laurie said and disappointment took root in her. Every window was dark.

"Let's go back to the building and ask questions. A former neighbour may know where she lives. Maybe she moved to another building in the area."

They returned to the address on Lottie's chart. The first two people they questioned didn't know her. The third man looked at them with suspicion.

"You from a collection agency?"

"No," Paul said. "I'm a doctor from Aurelia Memorial Hospital. Lottie hasn't been in to the clinic for a long time. I want to talk to her about coming back for treatment."

"They moved away months ago," the man said. Willing to provide information now. "It must have been over a year since they lived here. They had a bad car accident up in South Carolina. Their little boy was killed and Lottie lost the baby she was carrying. The way I hear it, she wasn't right in the head after that."

"Do you know where they live now?" Paul asked. Laurie knew his excitement matched her own.

"Can't say that I do." The man shook his head.

"Gus came out here late one night with a truck and a buddy of his, and they moved everything out. Didn't tell anybody where they were going. They were feeling pretty bad. Losing their kid and the one on the way, and Lottie not being right in the head."

"Did they have any special friends in the building?" Laurie tried.

"They kept to themselves most of the time. She worked at County General. The kid was in a day nursery."

"What about her husband?" Paul wanted to know. "What kind of work did he do?"

"Gus drove a truck." The man's face brightened. "I heard he got a real good job just after the accident. Driving one of those big deals that go on long distance hauls. Lotta money in that."

"Do you know which company Gus worked for?" Paul asked.

"No." He was regretful. "But it was one of the big ones." He squinted in thought for a moment. "Yeah, I remember now. It's that place about a mile down the highway. To the south."

"Thanks." Paul reached for Laurie's arm. "Let's move!"

Chapter Twenty-Seven

Lottie lifted the lid from the pot of slowly boiling black-eyed peas and dipped a spoon into the mixture. She blew on the peas, then cautiously tasted them. They were soft enough to eat. She turned off the burner under the peas and pulled open the oven door. Nothing ever baked just the way she wanted it in the old kerosene stove.

The molasses pie looked done. She took it out of the oven and put in on top of the stove to cool. She set two places at the table. When was Gus gonna leave on the California haul?

He kept carryin' on about how crazy he was about her. But he wouldn't let her get pregnant again. She didn't want him to keep bringin' her dolls. She wanted her own doll-baby, that she'd carry in her stomach for nine months. She also wanted a child to replace Junior, that's why she had to take the children.

She looked at the salt pork. It was crisp and brown on one side. She flipped it over on the other side. She could make the cream gravy in a couple of minutes. Gus was still upstairs in bed. He musta gone through that whole pot of coffee she took up to him. Not that it would stop him from eatin' like a horse.

She debated a minute, then decided to climb the stairs to tell Gus to come on down to eat. She was uneasy about shoutin' up the stairs with Tyrone sleepin' in the attic. He wouldn't wake up till the medicine wore off, though. Still, she was nervous about the noise.

"Gus . . ." She opened the door to the bedroom. Her face impassive. Her voice cool. Gus knew she was mad at him. "You come on down to the table. The pork's ready. It won't take more than a couple of minutes to make the gravy." She avoided looking directly at him.

"You got a good fire goin' in the stove?" He stayed under the mound of quilts. How could a man as big and heavy as Gus complain about the cold the way he did?

"I got plenty of coal in the stove. And it's warm from the oven. You come on down."

"Right away." His voice was cajoling. "Take that down with you." He pointed to the coffee pot. "Got any beer in the fridge?"

"Two or three bottles," she told him and reached for the coffee pot. Empty, like she'd expected. Gus drank more coffee than any man she ever knew. "You get your butt down to the kitchen, you hear?"

Lottie went out into the hall and down the stairs. Subconsciously she listened for sounds from the attic. When was Gus goin' out again? *She wanted him to leave*. Then she could bring Tyrone downstairs. Gus wasn't gonna take Tyrone from her. He was her little boy now.

In the kitchen she shifted the pork to a plate, leaving some of the fat in the frying pan. She stirred in the flour and blended it, adding the evaporated milk she kept around for gravy. Stirring the mixture. Put in some tabasco, she reminded herself. Gus would complain if the gravy didn't have some kick to it.

Gus came into the room and sat at the table. He stared at the pie sitting on top of the stove.

"That a molasses pie?" he asked with interest.

"It's a molasses pie." After the way he behaved before, why did she bother makin' anythin' special for him? Her kewpie doll face set in a rebellious pout.

Gus's eyes followed her movements as she brought the pork and then the black-eyed peas to the table.

"Honey, you know what the doctor said about you not gettin' pregnant again."

"So I won't get pregnant." She shrugged her shoulders. "But I think it's real mean."

All at once he seemed suspicious. "Lottie, you ain't up to somethin'?"

"I ain't pregnant, Gus." She stared accusingly at him. "You think I been messin' around with another man?"

"I know you ain't, honey."

"Maybe I ought to," she flung at him. "Plenty men would be glad to oblige me." But she had her Tyrone up in the attic. Gus didn't know about that. He'd never find this one.

"When you get your head together, and the doctor says it's all right, then you'll get pregnant," Gus promised. But Lottie saw he was nervous. He didn't know about Tyrone – he was just scared. "You're due to go back up to see that doctor near Charleston next month," he reminded. Every four months Gus took her up to see the doctor. She hated all the questions he asked. She never took the medicine he gave her. Gus didn't know she always threw it down the toilet.

"I don't want to go up there anymore," Lottie told him. "I don't need him no more." She brought a bottle of beer to the table and sat down.

"You need the doctor until he says you don't," Gus said sternly.

"When you goin' out on that California trip?"

"You keep askin' me that," Gus shot back. "What's so important about when I'm goin' out?" He hesitated, looking hard at her. "You ain't gonna do *that* again?"

"I don't know what you're talkin' about," she lied.

"You know." His tone was menacing. He'd had all he could take of that craziness. Her bringin' home brats and him havin' to get rid of 'em. "Lottie, you didn't go out and steal another kid?"

"You hear any kid in this house?" she challenged. "Every time you come back from a trip, you run into the other bedroom and look." Her eyes filled with tears. Every time he found her baby, he took it away. Times like that she hated him. But he wasn't gonna take Tyrone.

"Maybe I oughta look some place else," Gus said with sudden intuition. "Lottie, if you took another kid, I'll beat the hell out of you! And then I'll take the kid out and shoot it!" Gus pushed back his chair and lumbered to his feet.

"Gus, where you goin'?" Lottie screamed.

"To go through this house and make sure you ain't done somethin' crazy again!"

Chapter Twenty-Eight

Laurie and Paul raced back to the car. The density of the fog had grown worse. They would face slow driving tonight.

"Paul, do you suppose the Johnsons moved out of the state?" Laurie was apprehensive. "The man in their building said the accident was up in South Carolina."

"They could have been up there on a vacation." Paul backed out and swung about towards the road. "Let's try that trucking firm and see if Gus still works for them." Laurie felt the tension in Paul. He felt – as she did – that they were close to finding Tyrone.

"Should we stop somewhere and try to reach Ted or Bill?" They couldn't try to bring in the police; they were working on instinct. No evidence. Just this uncanny feeling that with every passing moment they were moving closer to Tyrone. *Let them find him alive.*

"We can't waste time, Laurie." Paul hunched over the wheel, straining to see the exit from the grounds. He moved onto the road. "The trucking firm is to the south of the highway. Right?"

"Right," Laurie confirmed. "About a mile."

"OK, let's watch for it."

They moved onto the highway. The tail-lights of the car ahead were a beacon for Paul to follow. He kept a safe distance, his eyes fastened to the circles of red that gave him direction. At intervals his eyes moved to the dashboard to check on distance.

"I never knew a mile to seem so long," he said.

"There it is!" Laurie spied a sign that pierced the fog. "On the left."

Paul swung off the highway and pulled to a stop.

"The place looks closed up." Laurie gaped in disappointment.

"The office is closed," Paul pinpointed and opened the door on his side. "Let's go around to the back . . ."

They hurried past the darkened office and the pulled-down metal doors of the adjacent structure. Paul reached for Laurie's hand as they swung around to the side of the large structure.

"Lights in the back," Paul noted with excitement.

They walked past half a dozen trucks parked outside for the night. At the rear a wide garage door was open. A couple of mechanics were working on the motor of a truck.

"Excuse me . . ." Paul headed inside the garage.

One mechanic paused in his efforts. "The office is closed for the day."

"I realize that." Paul concealed his impatience. "But it's terribly important that I talk to someone in charge about one of your drivers. It's a matter of life and death." The mechanic lifted his eyebrows in scepticism. "I'm Dr Norman from Aurelia Memorial." He pulled out his wallet and walked to the mechanic with ID extended. "Can you give me a phone number where I can reach your boss?" But their boss would not have addresses of employees on tap, Laurie realized in a surge of desolation.

"He's here." The mechanic surprised Paul and Laurie. "Mr Oswald!" he yelled towards the darkened area of the enormous shed. "Somebody here says he's gotta see you." The mechanic pointed towards a path between trucks. "He's in a private little office all the way down there."

"Thank you."

Laurie and Paul threaded their way between the trucks towards the faint light that shone from an enclosed cubicle beyond.

A small, heavy-set man with glasses stood in the doorway.

"You want to see me?" He was wary. "The office closes at five."

"We realize that." Paul was deferential. "I'm Dr Norman from Aurelia Memorial. It's urgent that I reach one of your drivers. Gus Johnson. His wife and he have moved from the address we have on file at the hospital."

"Gus sick?" He was astonished.

"No, Gus is fine. But his wife needs medical attention." He paused an instant. "This is a life and death matter. We have to reach her tonight." Paul wasn't lying; he wasn't misusing his profession, Laurie mentally defended him. Tomorrow Gus might kill Tyrone.

"I have the addresses in the office file." He reached inside the cubicle for a ring of keys hanging on a nail.

171

Together the three hurried through the shed and out into the night. While they walked to the office out front, the head of the trucking firm talked about his fourteen-year-old son who hoped to attend medical school.

"He comes home with all 'A's," he said with pride. "I keep warning him it's tough to get into medical school, but he says he'll get there. One way or another. He won't even talk about doing anything else. Stubborn, like his mother."

"That helps." Paul was gentle. "If he wants medical school and his grades are good, I'd bet on his making it."

Laurie and Paul stood by while he unlocked the office door, flung it wide, and reached inside for the wall switch.

"Come on in," he invited, already moving towards the files. He accepted the urgency of the situation.

Laurie tensed in the unexpected dank chill of the office, unheated in the evening. Paul reached to squeeze her hand in reassurance while they waited.

"Here it is." The head of the trucking firm pulled a card from the files. "Gus Johnson. He lives about eighteen miles out of town. All farms out there. I'll draw a little map for you." He pulled a pad towards him, found a pen. "It's kind of hard to find if you don't know exactly where to turn off. My folks used to own a place out that way so I'm familiar with it. I'm marking the turn-off just before the one you take, so you can be on the watch. With this fog tonight it's going to be rough."

Laurie and Paul listened while he gave them specific

instructions. Gus and Lottie lived on a rural road about eight miles off a county road.

"You won't see any street numbers," he warned. "But the mail boxes are all on one side of the road to make it easy for the mailman. Just look for a box that says 'Johnson'."

"We're very grateful," Laurie said while Paul took the map. "Good luck to your son when it comes time for medical school."

"Thank you ma'am." He grinned with pleasure.

Laurie and Paul returned to the car. He handed her the map.

"Keep your eyes on the directions." He fished in his jacket pocket and pulled out a tiny flashlight. "This'll help."

The fog had not lifted. The early evening traffic was heavy and moving at a snail-like pace.

"I wish to hell we could make some time," Paul grumbled while they sat still in traffic.

"We're coming to the turn-off before ours." Laurie read the road sign at their right. "It can't be far now."

At last they were off the highway and on the county road that would take them to the one on which Lottie and Gus Johnson lived. Here the traffic was very light. Laurie rolled down the window on her side so she could lean out and watch for signs.

It seemed an interminable time, though it was barely five minutes, before they arrived at the next turn-off. In this rural area there was no road lights to help them. Through the fog Laurie could see the expanses of open farmland. Then ahead of them lights showed faintly in a farmhouse set near the road.

"The mailboxes are on this side," Laurie said when they emerged from a dense patch of fog. "You'll have to go slowly now."

"In this fog I can't do anything else," Paul said ruefully. "I wish there was some way of knowing how far out they are."

All they knew was that the house where Gus and Lottie Johnson lived was somewhere on this road. They would have to keep driving until they approached a rural mailbox that read: 'Johnson'.

Chapter Twenty-Nine

Gus lifted the latch on the door that led into their dirt-floored cellar and thrust it open. Stooping because the space was too low to accommodate his height. He reached for the light cord and pulled it. Lottie hovered at his side. Clarence, his tail wagging in pleasure, waited for them to emerge.

"You satisfied?" Lottie demanded while Gus inspected the small, dank area that contained their potato barrel, a rusted plow, and odds and ends collected by Lottie's family for several generations. "Ain't nobody here."

"Let's go back into the house." Gus seemed mollified. "I gotta leave in the mornin'. We ain't stayin' up late tonight." Clarence barked, his eyes pleading with his master. "All right, you can come into the house," Gus agreed. "But you stay out of the bedroom. I don't want no dog hair all over my bed."

"There's still a chunk of molasses pie. You want it with some coffee, Gus?" Lottie wheedled. He wasn't gonna find Tyrone. He'd go away for two whole weeks, and she could play with Tyrone all she wanted. Her precious lil' baby.

"Might as well finish off the pie," Gus said. "And when did you know me to turn down coffee?"

They went back into the house. It seemed to Lottie that Gus was in a good mood. She couldn't wait for morning to come. Two whole weeks without Gus in the house!

"I'll put some more coal into the stove," she said while Gus dug into the pie. Clarence stretched himself in front of the stove. He'd be asleep in a minute. He loved comin' into the kitchen, Lottie thought, and practically roastin' himself here. But he wasn't no trouble when they let him in the house. When Clarence slept, a bomb couldn't wake him. "Gus, you left the Harley outside," she chided. He took it out when he went over to pay the grocery bill. "Bet you left the key in it, too."

"It's all right out here." Gus shrugged. "I don't like the smell it gets from sittin' in the barn." He gestured to Lottie to refill his cup. "I been thinkin'. I'm gonna buy that Franklin stove I been talkin' about for our bedroom. We'll use it plenty yet this year. We ain't had a winter this bad for a long time. You'd like a stove up there, wouldn't you?"

Lottie glowed. "That'll be swell, Gus." She'd like lyin' in bed, she mused, with the stove throwin' heat to the whole room all through the night.

"Go get the mail order catalogues," he ordered. Pleased with himself.

Gus waited for Lottie to bring over the catalogues. Her cherished winter reading while he was out on trips.

"I'll find it for you, Gus. I saw Franklin stoves in this one." She looked for the index, located the pages for the Franklin stoves, and flipped to the section.

When it came to buying things, Gus was good to her. He was only mean about her precious babies. "Here it is . . ."

Gus perused the offerings, debating about which model would best suit their needs and purse.

"All right, I'll order the stove before I leave," he decided complacently. "It oughta be here by the time I get back from California. I'll be able to hook it up myself. How much we owe on the credit card, Lottie?"

"Not much." All at once she was nervous.

"Lemme see the bill that just came in."

"It didn't come in yet," she lied. He mustn't find out that she bought a kerosene stove for the attic. *Then he'd know.*

"Sure it did." All at once he was guarded. "I saw it in the drawer there with all the other slips." He pointed to the drawer where they kept their bills. Lottie was proud that Gus always let her make out the cheques for everything, and he just signed them without asking questions.

"You saw somethin' else, Gus. The credit card bill didn't come in yet." She was stammering, the way she did when she was upset.

"Lottie, you're lyin' to me." Gus pushed back the chair and rose to his feet. "I always know when you're lyin'."

Lottie sat stricken, her heart thumping, while Gus went to the drawer and pulled out the bills. She saw him pushing through the slips that accompanied each delivery. The flannel nightgown she'd ordered. The sheets that were on sale. She liked pretty flowered sheets.

177

"What the hell did you do with a kerosene stove?" Gus demanded, his eyes fastened to Lottie.

"I didn't buy no kerosene stove." She was trembling. "We already got a kerosene stove."

"This ain't no cook stove. It's for heatin'. Where is it?"

"They made some mistake if they said I bought a stove. I didn't. They made a mistake. I'll tell them, Gus."

"You bought a kerosene stove, or you woulda told me they made a mistake when I come home!" He moved towards her. "You bought that stove to heat up some place in this house that I missed. You got a kid there. *Lottie, you did it again!*" His hand lashed out and slapped her. "I told you I'd beat the hell out of you if you took another kid! Where you hidin' it?"

"I didn't take no more kids!" Lottie wailed. "They made a mistake at the store." She broke into heavy sobs.

"I wanna know where he is!" He pulled Lottie to her feet. "I ain't goin' to jail for the rest of my life because you're off your rocker! I gotta get rid of him!"

"I didn't take no kid!" Lottie reiterated. "Gus, don't be so mean to me."

"Where is the kid? Am I gonna have to beat you to a pulp to find out?"

"Gus, no!" Lottie cowered before him. "Please don't hit me. Don't hit me, Gus—"

He clutched at her arm with a roughness that made her wince.

"You tell me where you hid it!"

"No kid in this house, Gus. I swear!"

"He's in this house, and I'm gonna find him." All of a sudden Gus's mouth fell ajar. Lottie could sense realization clicking into place in his mind. "You hid him in the attic! You bought that kerosene stove to keep it warm up there. That's why you been runnin' up to the attic all the time. Not for quilts. To that kid you stole!"

"No!" Lottie screamed. "No! Gus, where you goin'? Don't hurt him! Please don't hurt him!"

Chapter Thirty

Laurie leaned out the window as they approached another mailbox. The first in at least half a mile. She squinted, trying to read the name. 'Johnson'.

"Paul, this is it!" Her heart was pounding.

As he pulled to a stop, they heard a woman screaming. Her voice sharp and clear in the stillness of the night.

"Gus, no! You can't have him! Gus, don't hurt him! Please don't hurt Tyrone!"

"Laurie, drive back to the last farmhouse and call the police," Paul ordered, pushing open the door on his side of the car. "Tell them to make it fast! We've found Tyrone!"

"You can't go in there alone—" All at once Laurie was remembering how it had been with Mark. *She couldn't live through that again*! "Paul, no!" she called after him.

"Phone the police!" Paul reiterated, charging towards the house. "I have to stop him. I can't let him kill Tyrone!"

The front door appeared locked. Paul shoved with all his weight. The door gave way. He paused, listening for sounds. He heard the car driving away in a burst of speed. Laurie would bring help.

The woman screamed again. Somewhere on the upper floor. He darted for the stairs – subconsciously aware that a dog was barking behind a closed door on the lower floor. The woman began to wail hysterically. A man's voice yelled at her to shut up.

Fighting for breath, Paul hovered for an instant at the top of the stairs – seeking direction. Then his eyes settled on the rickety steps that led up to the attic. *They were up there.*

He raced up the stairs to the attic. Every second counted. No time to look around for a defensive weapon.

The other two had not heard him approach. They were fighting awkwardly – fiercely – in the low-ceilinged attic space. Hysteria giving Lottie an astonishing strength.

Paul spied Tyrone on the cot at one side of the attic. Asleep. Drugged, his mind told him. A kerosene stove close by to provide warmth. While Gus and Lottie were locked in battle, he scooped up Tyrone and headed back to the stairs.

"Hey!" Suddenly Gus was aware of an intruder.

"You leave him alone!" Lottie screeched, ignoring the intrusion. "You ain't gonna kill Tyrone! I won't let you!"

While Lottie threw herself again on Gus, Paul rushed down the stairs and out into the night. Shifting Tyrone in his arms, he stripped off his jacket to wrap around the inert small frame.

His eyes lit on the Harley parked beside the house. The key was there. *Thank God.* He settled himself on the seat with Tyrone in the protective custody of one arm. He had not been on a motorcycle since college, but this guaranteed them a fast getaway.

The Harley sputtered into action. Paul drove down towards the road with caution lest Tyrone slip from his grasp. He stopped short at an agonized cry that he knew instinctively had emerged from Lottie. He looked over his shoulder. The upper portion of the house had burst into flames.

Either Lottie or Gus had kicked over the kerosene stove, his mind told him. He deposited Tyrone – well wrapped in his jacket – on the ground and dashed back towards the house. The dog was yelping behind a closed door. He opened the door. The hound darted towards the front door, swinging wide now.

Paul tried to mount the stairs. A few steps up and he had to retreat. The heat was unbearable. No way he could make it up to the attic. The flames were shooting down the stairs, at his heels as he surged into the outdoors.

He picked up Tyrone and watched helplessly. The hound dog whining beside him. He heard a car approach, and another behind it. The first car was Angie's. Laurie emerged from behind the wheel.

"Paul, are you all right?" She was pale with alarm. Then she saw Tyrone in his arms. "Tyrone?"

"I'm fine. Tyrone will be all right as soon as he sleeps off the medication." He turned towards the blazing house. "Either Lottie or Gus knocked over a kerosene stove in the attic. I tried – I couldn't get up the stairs to bring them out."

"That house is just a pile of tinder." The man who had been driving the car behind Laurie's came forward.

"My wife always said it would burn down one night. I live in the house down the road," he explained. "We called the police. They'll be out here any minute." He hesitated. "I better drive back and call the fire department, too. We don't want that fire spreading into the woods."

Lottie's neighbour went back into his car and headed for a telephone. Paul deposited Tyrone – still oblivious to all that was happening – on the back seat of Angie's car.

"He'll be comfortable there until we can get him home," Paul said gently.

"What about you?" Laurie was anxious. "You must be freezing. Let's look in the trunk. Maybe there's a blanket there."

They found a blanket for Tyrone, and Paul retrieved his jacket.

"No more children will be murdered by Gus and Lottie Johnson," Paul said with quiet relief. "The nightmare is over. My only wish is that we could have questioned Gus and Lotty to find out the whole truth, and where the other children are buried, if only for their parents' sakes."

For a few moments Paul and Laurie forgot the burning house. Forgot Tyrone, asleep on the back seat of the car, Clarence slumped on the dirt road at their feet. They were engrossed in the pleasure of their first embrace.

"Oh!" Laurie pulled away after a satisfying interval. "I'm out of my mind!" She pulled open the front door of the car and reached into the glove compartment for the Nikkon.

"What are you doing with that?" Paul was puzzled.

"The article for *Manhattan Weekly*," Laurie reminded. "I need photos to go with my story." She began to shoot the burning house from a variety of angles. "Only one left," she sighed, hesitated, and spun around to Paul and snapped him.

"What's that for?" he asked in alarm. "Don't use me in your article!"

"That's for me." Unexpectedly Laurie laughed – while the sound of police sirens filled the air. "To keep me company until you come up to New York in April."